THE MASK OF APHRODITE

Dylan Connell

Legacy Book Press
LLC

Camanche, Iowa

Table of Contents

https://soundcloud.com/user-989024307/sets/mask-of-aphrodite-private/s-w7jQjCaw6YC?si=0c6f9debd1e34401b2ae7d45869064f0&utm_source=clipboard&utm_medium=text&utm_campaign=social_sharing

https://open.spotify.com/intl-es/album/6pGjwmGNHaqr3dyMYUqVpq

https://music.apple.com/us/album/mask-of-aphrodite/1728236450

Twins

Beauty walked blindfolded into the excess of the masquerade. Her elegance drew the eyes of all. Before being given the chance to fasten a mask upon her face, she was approached by Pain and Pleasure. The twins were charming and kind. It wasn't long before they captivated her full attention.

All around Beauty were hushed whispers. Her presence was not expected, and even more shocking was her bare face. These murmurs, however, were drowned out as soon as the sweet sound of symphony music resounded through the ornate hall.

Pleasure seized the opportunity, grasping Beauty's hand, guiding her from speech to dance with ease and rhythm, and stepping into the midst of euphoria. As the two swayed and twirled, they became fettered to one another.

The dazzling dance between Pleasure and Beauty became the envy of all the masquerade's observers. None was more envious than Pain, though. As the song climaxed, Pleasure held Beauty in the shelter of his arms—while Pain looked on—clutching tight the festering seeds of jealousy.

When the tune met its end, Pleasure eased his hold and whispered softly into Beauty's ear, "Excuse me for only a moment, I've been summoned by our host."

So, Beauty stood blindfolded and alone at the center of the masquerade. Until once again, the warmth of a familiar hand fell into her own...and simultaneously, the music resumed.

Still, this dance was Pain's, yet Pleasure and Beauty knew it not. And as the music went on, so did this cycle. Pleasure would return to see Beauty alone where he left her, then wander away, disappearing for this or that, and Pain would follow swiftly, so as to keep Beauty company.

Lotus Drinkers

The scorching sun sat in the cloudless sky high above the Spanish countryside. A continuous succession of wilting willows cast long creeping shadows on the dirt before Don Quixote and his squire. Sancho Panza leaned forward on his donkey to grab his trusty leather bota skin and filled his mouth with warm red wine. As the two descended into the valley, a clearing in the willows emerged, and rippling heatwaves blurred the path before them.

"Can we rest before the shade ends?" asked Sancho.

"Now?" replied the knight in dented armor. "No, I daresay rest is impossible. How can you dream of rest when the serpent stalks our every footstep? Can't you feel it? Its grip choking away the life force of the village we committed to saving?"

And with those words, he led his limping horse into the full light of day. His persistence was rewarded. For, dotting the horizon, was a water so clear and so blue that it could have been mistaken for the heavens—their first glimpse of the Mediterranean.

"Aha!" he pointed towards the sea, "it is just as the legends claimed, my dear Sancho. At the end of the path of willows will be a village shrouded in lavender mist."

"Espejismo," Sancho could barely believe his eyes. The island sat just off the shoreline with a thin purple cloud hanging inches above its sands. Rising above this haze was the outline of a village. The buildings' bright colors—when seen from a distance—blended into one, like the palette of a painter who has lost his mind. Still, as the two approached, the shades of the individual properties separated, and bloomed before them like spring flowers.

Between the island and Spain was a still figure that stood on top of the water, a young girl, unaffected by the steady rhythm of waves.

"How does she not sink?" asked Quixote.

The squire shook his head. He could give no answer until they made their way through the graveyard of abandoned boats that littered the beach across from Espejismo. Then, peering into the water, the explanation announced itself. Hiding just beneath the surface was a natural granite land bridge that ran from mainland Spain to the island.

"It must only function when the tide is at its lowest. See how it is already beginning to vanish under the sea?"

"Rocinante doesn't trust it," said Quixote.

It was true. Neither horse nor donkey would walk into the ocean without a bit of persuasion. So, the knight and squire were forced to step into the waters first and pull their animals behind them. The sea barely reached their ankles, but the mist rose to their knees.

The girl wore pigtails and had tan skin from long days of playing in the sun. She was taking flat stones from a small bag and skipping them.

"I'll never know how many I get," she said as her rock faded into the dense, lavender fog. Then she turned to look the two up and down and said, "There once was a knight so drunk with wine, he thought he'd met his lady fine, the sun forgot to shine and shine, and in the dark of night he kissed a swine."

"Ha! And what is your name young poet?"

"Gabriella."

"Well, I am Don Quixote de la Mancha: a knight, a gentleman, and a servant of the unprotected. My squire, Sancho, and I request room and board in your village while we prepare to battle with the monster that maintains a grip on your community. All in the name of Dulcinea: the inspiration for my exploits."

"Dulcinea?" she asked without moving a muscle.

"Yes, the sweetest, the most beautiful, the most divine in virtue: Dulcinea del Toboso."

"Oh, yes, you must mean the princess…" she trailed off as if she'd just remembered something important. "Well, I know nothing of monsters, but the princess is here in Espejismo. Every day, she visits the fountain of dreams and stares into her own reflection."

Quixote's eyes lit up like candles on a moonless night. He said to Sancho, "Did you hear that? Here! She's here."

Sancho nodded, thinking, *And what about the serpent?*

For Don Quixote though, this idea had already been replaced; infatuation consumed the mind of the knight. He tugged at the reins of his tired horse and pulled the limping animal across the bridge, into Espejismo.

"The fountain…" he roared at the townsfolk. "Where is the fountain of dreams?!"

The men, women, and children all looked at him with shock and confusion painted on their faces. Their eyes were gray, and they seemed more asleep than awake. Some burdened him with questions: "Who are you? How did you find Espejismo? Who told you of the fountain?"

The knight was in too great a rush to answer the questions of those who weren't dumbfounded and speechless.

Then he heard the soft voice of Gabriella behind him say, "Follow me, I know the way to the center of town."

The village was designed like a maze; the houses all appeared to be the same size and shape. Indeed, the only way to distinguish one building from another was by the change in paint.

Sprouting from the mist were thick, thorn-covered vines that ran up the walls and tangled around benches and lamp posts. Attached to these vines were lily pads that bobbed upon the surface of the lavender cloud like stars floating in the night sky. Each lily supported a budding pink lotus.

"What species of flower are these that mix the scent of syrup into that of sea salt?" asked Sancho.

However, as the words left his mouth, the street before them opened into the town square and Quixote's excitement took all attention away from his question.

"Dulcinea!" he shouted and paced the perimeter in long exaggerated circles. "Dulcinea, I have come for you!"

Sancho sighed and approached the fountain with his back to the sun. Water sprang from the top and descended into three pools, each larger than the last until it reached the base. The light struck the water at an angle, which made it glow rose-pink, the same color as the church that stood behind it.

In the center of the fountain was the origin of that plant which crawled into every free corner of the village; a knotted thicket of vines wrapped around the stone like rope. Sancho took a swig of wine and reached down towards the water to pluck a light pink lotus from the cluster of lily pads.

The severed flower pulsed in his hand like a heart. Sancho had never felt such vitality in a plant. Amazed, he reached back into the pool and grabbed for the source. Between the thorns, the vine throbbed in rhythm like an artery pushing blood through the body.

Meanwhile, the hysterical Quixote screeched like a magpie while he searched high and low for his idol. He checked in each of the surrounding alleys, peered into every open window, and finally stepped through the great chestnut doors of the church.

Gabriella—amused with his antics—followed the mad knight into the towering, pink house of worship.

"Dulcinea?" answered the priest, a tall, gray-haired man with a torso like a wine barrel. He was walking towards the odd pair, wiping pink stains onto his black robe with hands the size of dinner plates.

Gabriella went up to the man with whom she was familiar, and whispered in his ear, "He is looking for the blacksmith's daughter."

"Ah, but of course, the princess."

"You know her?" Quixote asked.

"All too well. After all, she is one of my most faithful patrons. I'm certain that she will return to the fountain when the sun sets. It is...her routine, you might say."

"Thank you, sir." Quixote took a step out of the church to examine the sky. He predicted the shadow of night would fall upon Espejismo in an hour, no longer.

"Yes, well, she's only a princess so far as… oh anyway, you'll find out for yourself," the priest trailed off as Don Quixote was already making his way back to the fountain.

The priest started again on his work, but after a moment of consideration, decided to extend his hospitality to the strange men in the plaza.

Sancho was still trying to make sense of the lotus when the shadow of the priest fell upon him. The man blocked the sun and fixed his dull, gray eyes on the plucked flower in Sancho's hands.

"These fountains flowers are sacred; they are not for the uninitiated."

"Ah, my apologies. I meant no harm—"

"It's quite alright," the priest remarked. Then he offered Sancho a cup and said, "Please though, if you are going to stay, I invite you to drink of our island's nectar."

The squire looked over to see that Don Quixote was already taking back the liquid in a single graceless gulp—one that was overflowing onto his armor. Sancho lowered his nose, the cup smelled like honeyed wine, but pink petals floated on its surface. He shrugged and took a small taste of the perfumed drink.

"Delicious," he said, smiling at the priest.

Then, as if the two were old friends and immersed in deep conversation, the priest said, "We know what the knight searches for, but what about you? What is your deepest desire?"

The question took Sancho off guard, and he paused to consider before saying, "An island just like this where I am king."

The priest wiped another pink splotch onto his black robe then put his enormous hand on Sancho's shoulder and said, "Ah! It is a good thing that you've found yourself here on Espejismo. Come with me. I'll see if I can make an arrangement."

Sancho looked at Don Quixote who was engaged in conversation with Gabriella and decided he may as well see what the priest could offer him.

Inside the church, Sancho noticed that there were no crosses, no statues of Jesus, and no religious iconography to speak of. He thought about asking the priest why this was, but decided it was better to stay silent than offend.

The priest led Sancho up a spiral set of stairs and onto a balcony. From this height, Sancho could see the sun approaching the horizon and watched with pleasure as the clouds flushed coral pink—like a reef above the Mediterranean.

"Finish your drink," the priest said, looking at Sancho's cup.

Sancho did not have much left of his sweet beverage. He did as he was asked and swallowed the petals in his last gulp. The sun was touching the sea now, half of its red body in and half out.

"Do you see it?" the priest asked and pointed out towards the horizon. "Your island—the island of 10,000 flowers?"

Sancho squinted, he wasn't sure he understood, and then…it was there, a mass of land just left of the setting sun.

"It's mine?"

"It will be soon."

Sancho let out a joyous cry that echoed in the town square. The exasperation caused Don Quixote to turn towards the church. It was then that he saw the princess. Dulcinea: wrapped in a dress the same color as the clouds, carrying her long golden hair behind her and gazing with penetrating blue eyes through the knight, as if he were made of glass.

"Oh, Dulcinea," Quixote stuttered and dropped to one knee, "please, I beg of you, tell me to believe what my eyes display before me. I have waited so long for you, my princess. Can you be true?" His vision clouded with tears, "No, it is impossible; you are nothing but a dream that has walked into my waking moments. Please… please, Dulcinea, do not deceive me. If you are not a figment of my fantasies—if you are real—know that I am here only to honor you in the highest way possible. To support you and to love you without end. I beg you Dulcinea, do not disappear."

"Do I look like an illusion?" Dulcinea asked with a confident smile on her face.

Quixote examined every detail of the middle-aged woman. Was she his muse? He was no longer sure. The image, which he had held forever in his mind, seemed as distant as his village, La Mancha. It was blurring with the woman that stood before him, mixing, and becoming as impossible to separate as God from creation.

He shifted from his kneeling position and stood up. He took two paces backwards and blurted out, "Prove to me that you are the princess."

"Ha! Prove to me that you are a knight."

Quixote grunted. There is so much that can be communicated with a grunt, but Dulcinea seemed not to hear it. Still, it mattered not, for the longer he looked at the princess, the more convinced he was that she was the object of his imagination—Dulcinea.

"And I have been waiting for you," she said, touching the knight's cheek. "Your legend has grown larger than life; your story has even reached our shores here on Espejismo." Then she reached into the fountain, grabbed a flower, and put it into her mouth. As she chewed the lotus, she took Quixote's arm and brought him to the water.

The knight and princess looked into their reflections and Dulcinea said, "Tell me what you see."

"It is too much; it will blind me," Quixote insisted and wretched back.

"Please," Dulcinea whispered and beckoned to him.

Then, Don Quixote stood before the pool and watched as his image transformed. "It is you and I," he began.

"Yes, I see that too."

"We are together, on a sailboat. You have your head upon my chest, and I have removed my armor."

"I've seen it a thousand times before," she whispered in the knight's ear.

"How? How can you have seen my dream?"

"It is the power of the fountain," Dulcinea said, and then she leaned in and kissed him. An inferno blazed within him like a spark after being set upon dry wood.

So it was that Don Quixote and Sancho stayed on Espejismo for five years. Each day, the two would drink the pink wine prepared by the priest; each day at sunset, Sancho would stand at the edge of the church balcony and peer out upon his island. Each day, Quixote and Dulcinea would walk hand in hand to the fountain of dreams and watch as their reflections metamorphosed into the images of their deepest desires.

Their teeth yellowed and their eyes faded into gray. Forgotten was the world outside of Espejismo. Each became lost in the twisted labyrinths of their clouded minds.

Still, the knight always wanted more—more wine, more lotus, more time before the fountain. He pressured the priest and began to receive a beverage at sunrise and sunset. When Dulcinea and Sancho learned of this, they protested until they too were served an additional ration. This trend continued throughout the village and by the time a double dose of lotus had become standard, Don Quixote was drinking a third cup in the middle of the day.

Between drinks of the potent cocktail, Don Quixote and Sancho divided their attention between two main occupations. First, they spent hours—sometimes whole days—in front of the chessboard. However, they moved their pieces with no ambition of achieving a checkmate. This was always done in silence and with great concentration. Neither side ever captured a piece of their opponent. They would only re-arrange the board, creating new patterns and then, without warning, inevitably become flustered and quit the game as it brought them shame to play it in the first place.

Their other diversion was the endless construction of a boat. They talked with ceaseless repetition about taking the vessel out to explore Sancho's Island. The boat, however, was never finished. Specifically, the knight and his squire could never agree on a final coat of paint.

First, Sancho painted it green. Then Quixote wanted to try red. Once Sancho's layer of green had been replaced though, he refused to step foot in the craft. Until, in the middle of the night, he applied a new layer of dark purple.

After that, a feud was established. Neither party was willing to compromise. So, instead of ever sailing the boat, the two men spent their days running around in circles changing its color.

However, this unvarying routine was entirely up-ended on the 7th day of the 5th year, when it was announced by the priest that—due to the increase in consumption—there was a shortage of lotus flowers.

At first, this was considered to be nothing more than a minor inconvenience—a mere triviality. After all, there was still red wine, fresh fish, and the fountain of dreams.

This mentality changed that first night without the sweet beverage. Every soul on Espejismo took note of the moonless sky. It seemed as though the God of sleep vanished from the island and its citizens were sanctioned to suffocate under the grip of insomnia.

For Dulcinea, the absence of the sweet, pink nectar was far more profound than she'd imagined it could be. She gathered every candle in the dark house, lit them one at a time, and watched as the towers of wax melted down until they were nothing but puddles. When one candle dwindled, she would laugh like the dancing flame told a joke that only she could understand, and then light another. She went on like this until the sun rose and she fell into bed to rest.

The next morning was full of frantic energy. Noise erupted through the streets and the townspeople buzzed about like wasps around a nest.

At noon, the knight stood shirtless before his bed watching the soft breaths of Dulcinea as she continued to chase a far-off sleep. Though her eyes were closed, he thought that she looked uncomfortable, as though her back was injured, and she was lying in a new position in order to avoid the pain. He put on his armor and went to the church to finish something he started years before.

"It's gotten away from me, and I can't be sure I'll ever get it back," Dulcinea said when she woke. She stood before the bedside window draped in nothing but a lavender sheet. Then she put her hands on either side of her ribcage and pushed on the empty void inside her chest, which she was sure would swallow her whole.

She stepped into the kitchen and filled a glass of wine to the edge. There was a single candle left on the dining room table. She took the wine like medicine, lit the wick, and held the new flame up to the window curtains. The ball of yellow fire got so close to the curtains that if even the slightest breeze directed it, it would have ignited the interior of the house.

When it did not, Dulcinea laughed again, refilled her wine glass, and walked to the beach. She couldn't remember ever seeing the tide so low. She pulled out long, thin, strands of blonde hair and let the tired wind sweep them away.

The lavender mist that had always surrounded the island was nothing but a thin cloud, burning off in the day's heat. She hid her face in her hands and was on the verge of weeping when she heard the quiet voice of Gabriella behind her.

"Please, there is something you must see. Please come with me."

She took the girl's hand and followed her to the center of town. When they arrived, a small crowd was gathered around the fountain of dreams; all eyes were fixed on the church's polished chestnut doors.

Without warning, the doors swung open and Don Quixote appeared, pushing forth an immaculate sculpture made of a material as clear as a window. The townspeople clapped and cheered. They had never seen a woman made of ice.

They surrounded it, wanted to touch it, and as the crowd swarmed the statue, Don Quixote and Dulcinea found themselves on the edge of the horde.

"It is beautiful," the princess said to the knight.

"It should be. It is you who is being represented after all, my darling."

"Me?" she asked, gazing upon the statue like a contorted mirror that only displayed a misshapen reflection.

"Yes, isn't the resemblance clear as day?" Quixote's eyes looked like cages. There was something struggling to escape behind their gray tint.

Dulcinea said nothing. She only gazed upon the statue. She sat on the edge of the fountain and stared until the crowd dispersed and only she and Quixote were left in the plaza. Quixote tried to speak to her once again, but the words never reached her ears. The ice statue put her under hypnosis, and nothing could break the trance.

Indeed, she sat before the statue all day—staring upon it without eating or drinking a thing—as if the image alone could nourish her. Eventually though, the statue melted away. First, it lost its form as a woman and became a clear unshaped mound. Then, as the sun began to fall towards the sea, it was reduced to nothing but a puddle.

Sancho Panza met Don Quixote before the church at sunset. The knight could not snap the princess out of her trance and so he joined Sancho and walked up the spiral staircase to the balcony.

When the squire looked off towards the setting sun, he asked himself, "Am I going blind?" Sancho leaned off the edge and looked as though he might jump towards the sea. Quixote grabbed his shirt collar and pulled him back.

"Fetch the priest," Quixote said to Sancho.

The squire wiped tears from his eyes and ran from the church. Quixote followed him out the doors and went back to the fountain. Dulcinea was crying too. She sobbed into Quixote's chest and as he looked upon her, he could not help thinking that her face seemed to be covered in a mask.

"What's wrong? What's wrong my darling?" and though she could not find the words to answer him, he sensed it too. A feeling hung between them like a phantom; an entity—though nameless— was pushing them apart.

"Come," he led her to the fountain of dreams. She was limp in his arms, and he was afraid that she would collapse if he set her down.

She did not though. She took her face from his chest and together they searched the still pool for their reflections, for the dream they shared together every night. After some time, an image floated to the surface. Still, it was murky, as though it was being viewed through a wine bottle in a drunken haze. The knight and princess knew what it was supposed to be, but the dream that had been so lucid for the past five years had faded.

A single tear fell from Dulcinea's cheek. It dropped from her face and collided with the fountain of dreams, causing ripples to disrupt the pool. After the splash, their muddled image never regained its prior form. In fact, it dispersed entirely from the impact of a single tear.

Don Quixote convulsed in fear then rushed Dulcinea towards the church. He kicked open the heavy chestnut doors and would have tried to carry Dulcinea up the stairs to the balcony, but he lacked the strength. Instead, she strode beside him, examining his face as if he had always worn a beard and just shaved for the first time in years.

The priest stood next to Sancho, whose eyes were fixed on the horizon like a child who was attempting to comprehend the complexities of a magic trick.

"There must be more Lotus!" Quixote declared.

"This is your fault you know," the priest said, turning from the setting sun. "You could never be satisfied and your cravings infected our entire island. Not once in the history of Espejismo have we run out of lotus."

"You are hiding it," Quixote spat back. "I know you are. Your eyes are still as gray as the day I met you."

The priest put his hands behind his back and looked down with shame. Then he said, "I confess, I saved the last of it for myself. There is a quarter barrel in the cellar, but I can assure you, there is not a flower left on Espejismo and there will not be again until the next harvest. It has been said… oh, well… no, that's nothing but an old story."

"The cellar?" Dulcinea asked, spinning around to retrieve what was left.

The priest nodded then Quixote asked, "What of this rumor?"

"Out there," Sancho pointed towards the sea.

"Yes," the priest continued his thought, "it has been said that Sancho's Island is covered in lotus flowers; flowers so sweet that the Gods save them for ambrosia and keep them protected from human hands."

"On Sancho's Island?" Quixote asked, as though he was unsure of his own memory.

"But where is my island?" Sancho asked.

"Yes, perhaps—" the priest began.

But he was interrupted by Dulcinea's return. She handed her knight and squire a cup of the sweet wine. They all drank as if it was fresh water and they'd been lost on the open sea.

When they finished, the priest said, "Perhaps it is easier for me to show rather than tell."

So, he led the knight and princess to the edge of the balcony and pointed out towards the setting sun.

"Sancho's island—the island of ten thousand flowers—do you see it now?"

"I see it," Dulcinea said first.

Quixote squinted and leaned forward, then finally he agreed, "Yes, I see it too."

"There isn't any time to waste," exclaimed Dulcinea.

"Yes," Sancho agreed. "We must sail today."

"The waters are dangerous my friends. There is no guarantee that the stories are true. Please, consider your actions before—"

"We must go at once," Quixote interrupted the priest.

The priest grabbed the knight by his shoulder and said, "Please, at least leave in the morning. I will meet you at sunrise with the last of the lotus and send you on your way. Do not depart on a night with no moon."

The three nodded in agreement and it was decided, they would leave the next day.

Dulcinea, Sancho, and Quixote met the priest by the water's edge just as dawn was bringing new light to the sky. He handed the trio the last of the wine and as they drank, the clouds above them turned flesh-pink.

Sancho made final adjustments to the sails and then the knight, princess, and squire pushed their half blue and half orange boat

through the lavender mist of Espejismo—west—towards the island they prayed could satisfy them.

All was perfect and serene upon the water. With his belly full of fresh lotus, Quixote lay down on the hull of the ship and let the warm sun close his tired eyes. He allowed himself to succumb to blissful apathy, to harmonize with the rhythm of waves pushing up against the boat.

Dulcinea joined Don Quixote, embracing him like a book does its pages. She held him tight, and their breath became one motion.

Sancho kept his attention fixed on the horizon and sailed in a straight line throughout the entirety of the day.

The sea faded into the sky and back again. Espejismo disappeared behind them. They ate separately without much talking and when day disintegrated, only stars dotted the black blanket of night—there was still no moon.

Sancho began to pace the length of the boat. "We should have reached it by now," he repeated. "We should have reached the is-land, and it has not moved. All day it has stayed fixed on the hori-zon, taunting us and...we should have reached it by now."

"Yes," agreed Dulcinea, "it looked so close from shore."

"By morning we will have more lotus than our cups can hold," said Quixote.

"Yes," they all agreed, "by morning."

Sancho tossed the anchor overboard and halted the boat's prog-ress. They began to drift aimlessly as darkness conquered the sky above them. Each individual retreated into silence. The air between Quixote and Dulcinea held the energy of an exposed secret that should have stayed hidden—the phantom had returned.

That night, there was no sleep on the boat. Though their eyes were heavy, and their bodies baked from the sun, insomnia ruled the sea. It wasn't due to lack of effort that the three were barred entrance from the realm of dreams. They turned about with restless thoughts that pounded in their skulls like drums inside of caves.

Dulcinea looked up at the stars like they held a message.

"What constellation sings to you?" Quixote asked.

"Hydra," she replied, tracing the figure of the water snake with her thumb and pointer finger.

"The serpent," Quixote said, "how could I have forgotten?"

When the sun rose, there was not a single cloud in any direction. Sky and sea were two mirrors placed face to face. The knight felt hollow, like there was nothing at all inside of him. He pulled himself off the deck and looked at Dulcinea as if she were a perfect stranger, "Your eyes are brown," he said.

"Yes, and they have always been so."

He shook his head, but before he could reply to this, Sancho shouted, "It's gone. Vanished. My island has evaporated like morning dew. What cruel trick is this? What God have I dishonored to deserve this fate?"

Dulcinea peered into Quixote's eyes with a look that read like a line of poetry. Then she turned away and refused to ever gaze upon him again. Quixote re-aligned his armor and said to Sancho, "Let us return to Espejismo. A serpent has coiled itself around that city like a noose around the throat of a sinner."

So, the trio sailed east. When they arrived, the lavender mist had vanished, and the air was clear. The townspeople moped about with sunken, sullen faces. They asked the three if they found Sancho's Island.

"No," they repeated.

Quixote followed Dulcinea one final time to the fountain of dreams. As they passed the church, Dulcinea stepped inside and took a lit candle from the open entrance. The plants heart stood beating in the center of the plaza. It was Dulcinea who tossed the smoldering flame into the soul of the lotus—the creator of apathy— the caster of illusion. The fire spread across the plant's vines like they were made of cloth. Quixote looked at Sancho and said, "The serpent has been vanquished."

Dom & Emmanuelle

"Dominique, oh, Dominique, my girl is so unique. I've never had a better one. She hides and makes me seek."

Emmanuelle sings as he shifts between 3rd and 4th gear, the sleek black Porsche swinging through the city like a shadow.

"You're the best thing that's ever happened to me. The best. I was so scared I'd lose you this morning. But you'd never let me go, would you?"

"Can you slow down?"

"New year, new us. Stronger than ever. Let's go over the bridge tonight. You're the poet. You should appreciate that. It's a metaphor. New year, new us. It's a symbol."

"Emmanuelle!"

Slams on the breaks. The engine sputters then stalls under the street lights' weak glow. A woman pushes a cart in front of the Porsche with bare, asphalt-black feet.

"Jesus fucking Christ, I'm driving here!" He honks his horn and, when there is just enough room, turns the car back on and speeds around her.

"What are you so…quiet for?" he asks.

Dominique looks out the window.

"You haven't said a word all night. Not a damn word since we stepped into that white bitch's mansion."

"I did try to tell you something."

"What?" Emmanuelle slows down in front of a red light and Dominique looks over at him.

"You know what," she says.

"Oh, come on! That? That was nothing. Just a little snort. You're not mad about that, are you? ...Dom? ...Dom? Are you? Ooohhh shit! Well, what did you want me to do? Everyone was playing with their noses. That was the whole point of the party. The second we left the bar, that was all that white girl could talk about. How she was gettin' enough powder for everyone to—"

"I know, but with the way we talked this morning. You didn't—I mean, you shouldn't have—whatever, never mind. Just take me home."

"Take you home!?" The Porsche screamed like a bullet. "What are you talking about? Are you crazy? I thought we were going over the bridge."

"Don't call me crazy."

"Okay, hey, I'm sorry. I'm sorry, babe. I shouldn't have said that. I shouldn't have done that. God, I shouldn't have done it. But you know me, Dom. Alcohol is my getaway. What did you expect from me? You put me in a room with all your friends, people I'd never met, and a bottle of Julio. I mean, what did you expect? Then, the rich white girl wanted to buy everything. I mean really, what did you expect? It's just as much your fault as it is mine. Shit. Fuck. Don't go home. Don't make me take you home, Dom. You know you're the most important person in my life, don't you? You know before you, I felt like I was sleeping. No, no, scratch that. This is the dream. It's just too good to be true. Don't wake me up."

"I don't want to go across the bridge. We've both had a lot to drink. I just want to go home and sleep."

There are almost tears, but Dom holds them in. Emmanuelle turns up the radio and exits for the freeway: I-80 Eastbound towards Oakland.

"Emmanuelle, what—the—fuck."

"Oh, come on, baby. That ain't right. You know that ain't right. I can't take you home now. Not before we fix this. Not before we fix us."

Dom digs her fingernails into the leather and reaches for a cigarette.

"What's the problem, huh? Cat got your tongue? You afraid of the big bad wolf? Ow, ow, owwooooo!"

"I shouldn't have even gone out with you tonight. I should have fucking followed through," Dom says more to herself. It is a thought she should not have let escape.

Now, it's Emmanuelle's turn to be silent. The Porsche speaks for him. 6th gear: 95, 100, 110 miles per hour.

"Please slow down," Dom begs. "I didn't mean it like that. You know I didn't mean I wanted—"

"What then? What did you mean?"

The bridge comes into view. Then, they're on it.

"Just that we shouldn't have gone out. You were right. It was my fault. I shouldn't have put you in a room with all those people."

"You're lying to me."

120, 125.

"No, I'm not lying."

"Yes, you are. You're trying to make me feel better. God, I'm a monster. You just want me to take you home. But once I do, I'll never see you again. You'll probably call your girls and tell them all what a basket case I am."

135, 140.

"Well, that's not going to happen!"

Emmanuelle thrusts up the emergency break. The Porsche drifts to the right. Dom's head knocks against the window. For a split second, she is convinced the car will flip over. But it doesn't. It screeches to a halt. Smoke rises from the tires and the road. There is no one else on the bridge.

Emmanuelle steps out of the car.

"What are you doing?"

He walks to the side of the road and looks over the edge.

"Emmanuelle, what the fuck are you doing?! Come back to the car."

Dom is behind him, in the street, running towards him. There are tears now.

"Please, please, I didn't mean it like that. Please, Emmanuelle, get back in the car. It was my fault, you're right. You don't have to take me home."

"This is what you wanted, Dom. I told you this morning this is what would happen."

He pushes her away. She swirls like a storm cloud and tumbles to the ground like rain. Blood from Dom's knee stains the concrete.

"Please, Emmanuelle, I'll never leave you. I swear to God, I'll never leave you. I'm always going to be by your side. Ride or die. We're gonna get you better. I know you don't want to hurt me. I know it hurts you to do it. You're not a monster. Please just get back in the car."

Emmanuelle steps away from the ledge. He picks Dom up and walks her towards the Porsche. They get inside, he starts the engine and drives at a steady pace.

"Dominique, oh, Dominique, my girl is so unique. I've never had a better one. She hides and makes me seek."

Ajedrez - Rosario Castellanos

Porque éramos amigos y a ratos, nos
amábamos;
quizá para añadir otro interés
a los muchos que ya nos obligaban
decidimos jugar juegos de inteligencia.
Pusimos un tablero enfrente
equitativo en piezas, en valores,
en posibilidad de movimientos.
Aprendimos las reglas, les juramos respeto
y empezó la partida.
Estamos aquí hace un siglo, sentados,
meditando encarnizadamente
como dar el zarpazo último que aniquile
de modo inapelable y, para siempre, al otro.

Chess

Because we were friends and sometimes we even loved one another;
Maybe to add another interest
To the many obligations we already had
We decided to play games of intelligence
We put a board in front of us,
Distributed pieces with equal value and ability for movement.
We learned the rules, we swore to respect them and began the game.
We were here doing this for a century,
Seated in intense meditation
Thinking about the final blow that will annihilate
The other forever

Ariadne on Naxos

Dionysus said he'd give me the sky. He told me he loved me the first time we kissed, and I knew then, that in his eyes, I could never be ordinary; I would always be perceived as art.

Dionysus fit me with a crown of stars. He called me his muse and reminded me as often as he could how thankful he was to be inspired.

Dionysus reversed my fate. Cherished me after I was abandoned by Theseus.

Theseus—the man who I led past the minotaur and out of the labyrinth—the man whose love I'd sacrificed everything for.

Theseus, who left me dreaming. Only to awaken on the island of Naxos—alone—black sails guiding our ship into dark maroon clouds. His rejection so heavy, I was sure my bones would break beneath it.

Dionysus wanted to rescue me from myself. He thought that if he showered me with endless gifts and poems, that I would be "cured."

At first, our love was a frenzy—a hysterical intoxication that absorbed my entire being.

Still, we are only capable of accepting the love in this world which we think we deserve.

So, when the fire of infatuation began to die down, a numb chill crept over me like the first frost of winter; I felt I deserved less and less.

I was fading away—disappearing—losing track of my *self* and vanishing into nothing.

Once the dark shadow of my melancholia began to overwhelm our light, Dionysus increased his efforts, but I only felt the worse for it.

I became so tired of disappointing him that I started to pull away and barricade myself in that darkness.

He must have sensed this too. Our amorous madness was gone. As our time together inched forward, I could feel The God who walked earth as man search for inspiration elsewhere.

A void grew between us. When he would stretch his arms across the abyss, I no longer had the strength to grab his hand.

My love turned to guilt.

Thus, when the harvest festival began on Naxos, I wandered from the crowd and into the vineyards. I did not want to be searched for; I did not want to be found.

Torch lights and music dispersed behind me.

I wished I could control that which I could not. Thoughts of my heart churned chaotically, as if mirroring the storm clouds which shaded the dark sky above.

First, came the noise of waves, then a vison of turbulent sea.

As my eyes gazed out upon the endless expanse of water, my feet became tangled at the earth.

Green grape vines wrapped around my ankles. I tripped, turned about, and tumbled into the thicket. Branches as strong as braided rope constricted my limbs. Struggle as I may, I was trapped.

I screamed into the lifeless night. The only response was the echo of my voice. What was I doing running away from what the world called: *true love*? Perhaps I deserved to be alone.

The heavens wept, and Zeus hurled angry purple bolts into the sea. Rain fell in dense, dreadful droplets that changed dirt to mud. Sinking deeper into the vineyards' clutch, I abandoned myself to the sisters of fate.

Hope came through the heavy rain in a luminous flash. A Pegasus and its rider being blown about by the wind. A winged white stallion crashing down on the island.

"Help," I cried, praying my voice would not be vanquished by thunder.

Perseus cut me from the vines.

Perseus, a mortal who'd beheaded a gorgon. Perseus who'd founded Mycenae and lay his enemies to waste.

Perseus, whose reputation for angering the Gods reached Naxos long before his sandals touched its beach.

In the cramped shelter of a low hanging cave, Perseus listened. I told him of love, of pain, of the desperate wish to feel anything at all, and of what it meant to be numb when that wish went unanswered.

What Perseus offered me was an option. He clutched the torn-off head of a woman whose hair was snakes. He declared it was written in the oracle: when the power to paralyze changed hands, the first sufferer of this curse would be divided.

And what did I have to fear? I was already stone. The love of Dionysus transformed me years ago.

Still, it took all of my will to conquer instinct and stare into Medusa's dull yellow eyes.

My body was turned forever into white marble. My soul split in two.

Half of me lived on as the daughter of Medusa, a gorgon who would seduce the like of women rather than men. This newfound freedom produced sensations within me which I never imagined possible.

Dionysus would find the other half of me. Frozen in time, frozen in his mind.

Dionysus went to war with Perseus and made a shrine of my statue.

Dionysus used wine to recruit the raving ones, his mad women, the maenads.

He took many to his bed. Unable to forget what he'd imagined I was, Dionysus never married again.

Instead, he adorned my figure with golden necklaces. He fit my wrists and ankles with bands and bracelets from foreign lands. He forced rings of sapphire, emerald, and ruby onto each of my fingers.

Gazing at the constellations from his tower's highest window, The God composed poem after poem in my honor.

I watched it all from fixed eyes.

Time was forgotten on the island. Sundials were cast into foaming waves. Measuring the cycle of the moon was a forbidden act.

Whole years passed without noticeable change. Empires rose and fell like the tides.

The palace degraded. The God of the grape came to be known by a new name, that of: Bacchus. Revelry and chaos consumed Naxos. A scarcity in wine could never be imagined.

One night, as the moon fell into the sea and the sky went black, Dionysus came to my relic and caressed my stone face. He spoke as if he knew I could hear him.

"Ariadne…"

The Cult of Venus

The first bang on my door came at 4:13 in the afternoon. I'd been in front of my screen all day, and just an hour earlier, I thought I was close to accomplishing my goal. Now the system was crashing. What I needed was a nap. My eyelids were heavy, and sleep was beckoning to me like escape to the prisoner. Then a second round of hammering erupted at my door. "For Chrissake," I mumbled as I stepped away from my malfunctioning computer.

"Just a minute!" I yelled. Whoever it was, they'd have to wait while I splashed my face with water and washed my mouth out with Listerine.

As I was covering my long curly hair with a Warriors hat, there was a third round of knocks at my door. I caught my reflection in a small mirror that separated the two sides of my coat rack and realized how angry I looked. I took a deep breath to compose myself before opening my door.

"Aha, Zamir, Zamir, Zamir. You look'a so beautiful. I could kiss your earth-brown skin." It was Palermo, my neighbor from across the hall, whose Italian accent always got thicker when he was excited.

"What's gotten into you? Why were you hammering on my door?" I asked the short man who wore Gucci loafers and covered his bald head with expensive fabric.

"Well, Zamir, I apologize for interrupting your precious Friday afternoon, but I have made a breakthrough on my most recent work of marblé. It is my opinion that an event like this calls for a celebration, don't you think it?" he asked, smiling up at me and showing his glittering golden molar.

"Sure, why don't we celebrate tonight?"

"Nonsense, I will not hear of it. Please, let me in, prepare some espresso, and we will share this fantastic blend of high-potency cannabis sativa, lavender, mugwort, and rose petals," he said, displaying a king-sized joint with his pinky finger sticking high into the air.

I was annoyed with Palermo but needed a break and didn't mind the idea of a midday smoke. Palermo and I celebrated the completion of his finished pieces together on my balcony four or five times before. He insisted that my perspective as a layperson was far more valuable than those of the elite art world's critics. The truth is, I think he's rather lonely, and I doubt his art has many admirers. I made like I was struggling with what to do before saying, "Fine, you can come in, but I don't have any espresso, only a French press."

Palermo stepped through the door, looked a little disgusted, then asked, "What about the cream, eh?"

"I have some cream, yes."

"Zamir, my friend, I can tell that you are tired; maybe you have had a long day or a long week. Of that, I am not so sure. I thank you for your hospitality and—to demonstrate my gratitude—I will make for you, the coffee with cream and sugar," he said, clasping his strong, pale palm on my shoulder and squeezing it before heading toward the kitchen.

I was still irritated with Palermo, but the edge of my emotion was being dulled by his high spirits. He began fumbling awkwardly with my French press, then looked up at me and asked, "So, how have you occupied your day prior to my arrival?"

I rubbed my eyes and yawned. "I was working on the software for the new Core X Processor, and something went wrong. It's like it took on a life of its own. I'll have to fix it, but—"

"Just a minute," Palermo said, interrupting me. "Where is the music? A beautiful moment like this needs the right music. Don't you think it?"

I pulled out my phone and turned on a nearby Bluetooth speaker. "Let me guess, you were thinking Vivaldi?" I poked fun at my guest because I was not convinced of his Italian heritage.

Palermo paused halfway through pouring steaming water over the grounds. "To be honest with you, in my mind, I was imagining Ottorino Respighi. But Vivaldi is a splendid alternative."

I decided to play one of Respighi's more obscure pieces to see if he would be able to tell the difference.

"This is a beautiful song," he said, pretending to conduct the orchestra with a stirring spoon. "Vivaldi accessed and amplified the emotions of his deepest soul, don't you think it?"

"Sure," I said.

"How much sugar you take? One or two?"

"Just one is fine."

"Good man. Come, let us smoke on your balcony. I want to tell you of my project."

Fog was rolling into the city, and the air outdoors was refreshing. I ignored the handle of my coffee cup and enjoyed its warmth in my palm.

Palermo struck a match to light his joint. He's the only person I've ever known whose preferred mechanism for generating fire is matches. He took three long puffs, followed by a swig of his coffee, and passed the smoldering work of art my way.

"So..." I said through thick bursts of aromatic smoke, "what's got you so excited about this project?"

"First, let me ask you a question, Zamir," he said, beckoning for the joint.

"If you must."

"Why do you think it...that the antiquated polytheist mythologies always include romantic relationships between their gods and goddesses?"

I took a sip of my coffee and swished the strange question around my head like the bitter liquid in my mouth. "Give me a second to change the music," I said, trying to buy some time before answering.

I pressed play on Herbie Hancock's *Head Hunters* album and took the joint back.

"A lot of stories in that time were used to explain natural phenomena that sparked people's curiosity," I said. "For example, Persephone is the daughter of Demeter, the goddess of agricultural harvest. So when Hades abducts Persephone to the underworld, her mother is overwrought with grief; consequently, her role as goddess of the harvest is neglected, causing a devastating winter. The conflict is brought to the attention of Zeus, who rules that Persephone is to spend half her time with Demeter on Earth and half her time in Tartarus with Hades. The story was used to explain the change of the seasons: Persephone was supposed to stay in the underworld for the six months of fall and winter. When she emerged, the whole earth would rejoice in spring."

"But isn't there...how you say it, something more? In some cases, don't the gods and goddesses represent metaphysical forces, with their union acting as a symbolic demonstration of harmony in nature?"

"I think that balancing act takes place more often between siblings," I said, knowing I was steering him away from his main point. "The most obvious example that comes to mind is Helios and Selene—literally sun and moon."

"Perhaps," he grunted, looking offended because I hadn't agreed with him.

"Were you thinking of a specific example?" I asked.

"Yes, but of course. I was thinking of the marriage between Venus and Vulcan."

I did a quick translation of the Roman names to Greek, which I was more familiar with. Had Aphrodite married Hephaestus? The joint must have been working because my memory regarding the subject was hazy. "Ah, have you fallen in love, Palermo?" I asked, avoiding the details of the myth.

"You've guessed it, but surely it is not the way in which you are thinking. Palermo, the sculptor, has been visited by Venus. Of this, there can be no doubt. But it is not a woman with whom I am enamored. Rather, it is a work of art—a creation of Hephaestus."

I paused to take another drag off the joint that was reaching its end. "I see," I said, despite my uncertainty. "So . . . you've fallen in love with your sculpture?"

"Not quite exactly. First, I fell in love with an idea. Taking place in the studio of my imagination some twelve years ago, I created the perfect woman. There has never been a woman in the world more beautiful, of that I can assure you. Then, as a labor of my devotion to her, I spent much of my free time over these twelve years attempting to recreate the image I had in my mind. Truthfully, I will tell you that it was a million failures. My human hand could not replicate the form I saw in my imagination because any perceptible flaw was intolerable. Much like Vivaldi, I could not settle for less than what existed in my truest heart."

"But today, you've made a breakthrough?" I asked, suppressing my desire to laugh over both Palermo's imagined classical expertise and his surface-level notion of the perfect woman.

"Today, I have overcome the greatest obstacle of all. For years, I was unable to give justice to my statue's eyes."

"Until today?"

"Precisely, Zamir. Until today."

"Well, I'm glad you found love. And in this city, it's far from the strangest relationship I've heard of." I laughed and patted him on the shoulder.

"Come on then, don't you want to see her?" he asked, tossing the roach off my balcony.

"Damn it, Palermo, I've told you not to throw anything off my balcony. I have an ashtray." I scowled at him.

"It is beside the point, my friend. Come, come, you will be the first, besides myself, to set eyes upon her," he said, standing up and sliding by me. "*Permesso, grazie.*" He made his way into my living room, set his cup by the sink, and cocked a stoned, sideways smile my way.

I was feeling pleasantly buzzed as we floated across the hall to Palermo's cluttered studio and gallery. I'd never actually been inside

Palermo's apartment before; it smelled like wet clay and was nearly full of statues. Some of the pieces were surely too large to fit in our elevator; plus marble is heavy. *How the hell did he get all this up here?*

I might have smoked too much, I thought upon entering his private space. Sweat was crowding my palms, and I was giving extra attention to the rapid pace of my heartbeat. In front of his bedside window was the form of a statue covered by a thin white sheet. Palermo strutted confidently in its direction for the unveiling.

"Ta-da!" he announced as he pulled the veil back on his marble statue.

I hadn't expected her to be as beautiful as he'd boasted. The proportions of the body were divine. The hair was shoulder-length and curly, the lips round and full. Still, most intriguing of all were the dark orange eyes, which looked out from the stone with a melancholy understanding. I was awestruck.

"Palermo," I finally stuttered. "This is wonderful."

"Wonderful, ha! She is far more than wonderful. Pay attention to her eyes," he said, then began waving his hand in front of the statue's face. To my surprise, her apricot eyes seemed to be following his movements.

"That's quite the effect," I murmured.

"I have endowed her with an implant," Palermo said, pointing toward the back of her head. "Behind her eyes are motion-detecting sensors."

"How long did it take you to figure that out?"

"Twelve years...twelve years of fixing every single detail. But it was all worth it. She's the best statue I ever created, and she's all mine," he said, on the verge of tears.

"You don't plan on selling the piece?"

"Never, not in a hundred thousand rotations around the sun. I made her so that I could enjoy her perfect beauty. I made her so I could be with her day and night," he said, stroking her hair.

"Well...she really is perfect, Palermo." I didn't know what else to say. I couldn't take my eyes off the statue, and the idea of a man falling in love with a piece of marble was sounding less and less insane. "Have you named her?" I asked.

"Ah, I am glad you ask it. She has always been my Giuliana."

"That's beautiful," I said, my eyes still fixed on the statue. *I wish she were mine,* I thought.

Then, almost as if sensing my reaction, he picked up the sheet and concealed his masterpiece. "I thank you for coming over," he remarked. "And for celebrating with me on your balcony."

"Thank you for having me," I smiled. Had he gained insight into my jealousy?

"We will have to do it again sometime soon. But next time, you make the coffee for me."

"That sounds fine, whenever you want."

"Good." He was walking me to the door now. He must have sensed my reaction.

How embarrassing, I thought. Better to just play it off like nothing happened. "Well, I'll see you around."

"Surely!" His golden tooth glimmered back at me, and then his door shut.

II

I stood in the silent hallway for a brief moment. I wanted to go back into Palermo's bedroom and sit in front of the statue until it whispered the secrets of love to me. I wanted to touch it, kiss it, and look deeply into its lifelike eyes. This was, however, impossible; I doubted whether he would ever let me, or anyone else for that matter, view the statue again.

Instead, I returned to my apartment, closed my eyes, and tried to commit the image to memory. I needed to see her again. Knowing she was so close and yet completely out of my reach would drive me mad before midnight.

With closed eyes, my imagination was like a lucid dream. Palermo was always mixing strange herbs with his marijuana. I hadn't given the blend a second thought before smoking it. But as I tilted my head back and allowed my mind to obsess over the image of the statue, I wondered if we hadn't smoked something a bit stronger than lavender and rose petals.

Synesthesia. Everything was colorful, and the brightest image of all was Palermo's statue, luring me in. Then, a call to my cell phone interrupted my trance. *Shit, is it really 6:45?* I thought, remembering I was supposed to be meeting friends from work.

"Hello," I answered on the last ring.

"What's up? Are you coming out tonight?"

"Damn, the day's gotten away from me. My processor is fighting back. I've got to do some serious damage control, or you may not see me in the office next week."

"Zamir—" a loud crash in the bar's background interrupted him. "Oh, come on, bro. It's going to be a good night. Everyone's here, and Alexa's been asking about you."

I tried to conjure up an image of Alexa from our company's sales department. My friend knew about my long-standing crush on her, but for some reason, I was unable to remember what she looked like.

"Sorry, you know how I am… Once I start something, I've got to finish it."

"Whatever. Suit yourself, then. I'll see you Monday morning. Peace."

"Peace," I said, then hung up the phone.

I really should check on the processor, I thought. And anyway, I felt strange. I didn't want to make a public appearance with the swarm of questions buzzing about my head.

Still, I was past wondering if it was possible to feel infatuation for a statue. I wasn't able to explain why it was happening to me, but there was no question that it was happening. A part of me lectured, calling my feelings for an inanimate object "sick and unnatural." But this voice was smothered every time my mind recreated her perfect image.

"What am I doing?" I asked the empty room.

I went back to my desk and attempted to settle into my work. The Core X Processor was essentially a code cracker. I was employed by the Blackrock Corporation and they wanted a program that used artificial intelligence to break through security systems. For the right price, I was sure they would be willing to turn around and sell my work to the military. I wasn't getting paid to ask those kinds of questions, though. So I kept my mouth shut and coded.

The program went rogue. While I was distracted by Palermo, it broke through the building's firewall and was now spitting my neighbor's data back at me like I'd asked for it. Worse, it was spreading through my neighborhood, consuming the digital information of everything in its path. It dawned on me that my program was breaking the law, so I froze it. The processor resisted, but I was able to halt its progress before it got out of my control.

When I settled it down, I noticed something else peculiar: the program also mined my data. I began to investigate what personal information it stored and was horrified. The processor didn't just collect my search history or categorize my electronic purchases. No, it stole everything: my text messages from seventh grade, my list of secret obsessions, even diary entries about failed relationships that I'd made without a journal nearby. And it was doing something with the information—a synthesizing, a spreading that was out of my hands.

The program took my most personal information, rearranged it, and transmuted it. It was all too much for me to observe. A disorienting feeling overtook me, and as I stepped away from my computer, I felt as though I were entering a scene from a painting. Colors were too bright, and the sound of my music was bursting with vitality. I could see it—I could actually see the music—bouncing around my room like fractured waves of light.

I'm exhausted, I told myself and rubbed my eyes. *I've been working too damned hard. I'll pick up where I left off in the morning.* Then, the memory of Palermo's and my conversation regarding Aphrodite and Hephaestus roared up at me like a fire from a heavily greased pan. I went to my bookshelf, pulled out my worn hardcover copy of Edith Hamilton's *Mythology*, flipped to the index, and located Hephaestus's name.

A brief introduction was made on behalf of the god's gnarled limbs, his talents as a blacksmith, and the ancient society's approach to worshipping him. It also mentioned that the identity of the Olympian's wife changed depending on the text. Citing that she was "one of the three graces in the *Iliad*, called Aglaia in Hesiod; in the *Odyssey,* she is Aphrodite." This was all we got to know about his marriage.

Nearby was a copy of the *Odyssey* that I highlighted and scribbled in as a freshman in college. The index directed me to a side story in chapter eight of the epic. This tale dealt exclusively with the marriage of Aphrodite and Hephaestus. Now I was getting somewhere. I brought the book with me to my red velvet reading chair, turned on my overhead lamp, and switched the music over to let Stanley Turrentine blow on his sax for a while.

I'd written 'Odysseus = champion competitor' next to the text, and the note triggered my memory. Homer's protagonist was demonstrating his superior athletic talents in a competition on Phaeicia. His toss of the discus wowed his fellow competitors and the island's king, Alcinous. Then the king called for a bard, and I had no memory at all of the events that followed. The brand-new story animated my imagination with the same intensity that visited my earlier daydream. I was no longer in my apartment or, for that matter, in San Francisco. My mind's eye was transported to the front row of an Athenian theater, and the gods were actors in the ensuing play.

I barely noticed as handsome Ares entered to the left of the set; my focus was directed toward Aphrodite. She was flawless perfection—the marble statue from Palermo's bedroom, yet a thinking, speaking, and acting replica.

But why was Ares showering Aphrodite with gifts? And why was she accepting them along with his physical advances? This was supposed to be a story about hobbled Hephaestus and his love for Aphrodite, the most dazzling goddess of all. Yet, it was the personifications of Love and War who were intoxicated with passion. They embraced, became lost in each other's arms, and disappeared into a great iron bed.

After the amorous vanishing act, a thickly muscled mountain of a man limped on stage. He was accompanied by another so bright it seemed as though someone went to the trouble of attaching mirrors to his clothing. I took them to be Hephaestus and Helios, lord of the sun.

Helios spoke first, "I spied the couple. I speak to you truly when I say I witnessed them in the act. They have shamed you and defiled your home in the process."

Hephaestus recoiled as if an anvil dropped upon his chest. "If it is so, then I must enact my revenge."

"So be it. But I warn you, be careful with that brute Ares. He's got the temperament of a cornered bull and the strength of a thousand lions," Helios counseled.

"Of this, you speak the truth as well. I must seek my vengeance on my own terms," he said, nodding to Helios, who took his cue and departed. Afterward, Hephaestus got straight to work crafting thick chains. The type that seemed as though they would be near impossible to slip through or break. Hephaestus was a spider spinning a web; he wove the chains around the very same iron bed that Love and War shared.

When his trap was complete, the living marble Aphrodite waltzed onto the set with confidence in each step. "Darling, you seem distracted," she said, running a finger across his broad back.

"It is my latest work," Hephaestus replied. "I must leave for a week's time to complete it."

"It is always your work." Aphrodite's speech turned cold.

Hephaestus averted his eyes from the marble beauty and limped off stage. Moments later, the glistening, tall, and strong-faced Ares replaced him, passing gifts and kisses to the cheating spouse. The cherry red of Ares's garments swirled in combination with Aphrodite's dark, honeyed shade. The vortex of lust twisted and turned all the way to the great iron bed. Ares picked Aphrodite up and held her in his powerful arms. They fell, lips to lips, into Hephaestus's web of chains.

Only then did Hephaestus limp back onto center stage, engage the trap, and address the couple: "A sad day for adultery, tsk-tsk."

Ares thrashed about, cursing and threatening the god of the forge. Aphrodite, on the other hand, froze. She returned to the stillness that defined her existence as a statue in Palermo's bedroom. She was just beginning to weep as the metamorphosis consumed her. Our eyes locked as the first tear dropped to her cheek, and then she stiffened like a corpse.

All around me was cheering and laughter. I was no longer the only spectator in the theater. Hephaestus caught his wife with a lover and put them on display for the rest of the Greek Pantheon. Revenge burned in his eyes like the fire in his forge. Aphrodite looked out at me—paralyzed eternally by shame.

III

At that moment, there was a buzzing in my pocket. The theater of my imagination crumbled, and my psyche returned to the air-conditioned library of my apartment. *Whatever we smoked was definitely stronger than grass,* I thought.

The text turned out to be from Palermo. "Dear Zamir," it read. "I want to apologize for rushing you out of my apartment this afternoon. The marijuana had me feeling...unnaturally anxious. I needed to be alone in order to collect myself; I hope you understand. Perhaps sometime this week, we can talk again. Ciao, Palermo."

He was the only person I knew who wrote texts like they were formal letters. I typed up a reply in all caps. *WHAT THE HELL WAS IN THAT JOINT, PALERMO!?!?* But I slid my phone back into my pocket before sending it. Instead, I went out to my kitchen and boiled some chamomile tea. Everything would be better after a night's sleep. *I just need to calm down and get some rest,* I told myself.

It was nearly eight o'clock, and the sky was glowing cherry red and swirling with dark honeyed yellow. I went out on the balcony with my tea to better admire the sunset. My whole neighborhood seemed to be preparing for a celebratory Saturday night. Restaurants were full, live music was being played in the streets, and a thin fog hung in the balance between the earth and sky.

As the sunset's colors evaporated and my tea began to dwindle, I noticed a bright orange star hanging above the fog just west of me. It seemed so close that if I reached out, I would be able to grab it. I pulled my phone from my pocket and opened my Stargazer app. I pointed the camera in the direction of the bright bulb and then waited for the all-knowing power of technology to generate an answer as to what celestial body I was admiring. I shouldn't have been surprised when the result came back: Venus in peak.

I laughed for a moment, went back inside, finished off some leftover pizza, tidied up the kitchen, and decided to get to bed early. I laid my head down, hoping to free my overactive imagination from the commingling images of Aphrodite and Palermo's statue.

Sure enough, I was asleep within minutes. Still, it was far from peaceful rest. I was met in my dreamscape by the teary-eyed statue of Aphrodite. She was as still as Giuliana when I left her in Palermo's room. As still as she'd been after Hephaestus exposed her in the theater. I made my way over to her, wishing to caress her, to feel her flawless surface, and press my lips to hers. But a force beyond my control held me back. Nevertheless, I was content just to hold her gaze. Indeed, it was more than I could ask from such divine beauty.

"Set me free—you, you, you—set me free," her voice repeated, despite her lips staying sealed.

"How?" I asked. Then there was silence.

We stared into each other's eyes for the timeless eternity that only dreams can provide. Then, with no warning whatsoever, she spoke, "Awaken, Zamir."

Young dawn and her rose-red fingers painted a new day on the sky's canvas. I lay in bed feeling just as strange as the night before. My heart sang a song of obsession that only the earliest stages of love can produce. My mind reminded my heart that these feelings were directed toward a marble statue owned by my next-door neighbor. *You can't love an object,* I reasoned. *It's lust at most.* Still, the heart rarely listens to the mind when matters of passion are involved, and so the winged creature sang on from the center of my chest.

I went into my kitchen, drank a cup of black tea, and decided it was time to go ask Palermo exactly what he'd spiked the joint with. However, before I could cross the hallway and knock on his knotted pine door, he burst into my apartment like a gust of wind.

"Gone! She is gone! My Giuliana, she is missing!"

"What do you mean, missing?" I asked, my heart swelling.

"Is it not self-evident?" He threw his silk cap onto my tiled floor. "She has been stolen. I woke to this new day, and my statue—my prized possession—was nowhere to be found. There is only one man to blame."

"I hope you don't mean me," I replied.

"It could have been no one else. You are the only soul who has connected with my beautiful creation. I saw the way you gazed upon her. There was lust in your eyes."

"Think, Palermo. No one could have gotten in or out of your apartment unless you authorized it. You have a security system fit for a senator," I said.

He paced back and forth before saying, "Yes, but you're the one with, how you say, technological expertise."

"And?" I said, thinking about the processor.

"You must have broken in. You have the network, the sophisticated tools..." He paused and hid his face in his hands. "I just want her back. All I want is to have her back in my life."

"There is one possibility," I said, thinking of the implant.

"Yes?" he looked up with pleading eyes.

"How do I put this...Last night, the system I've been working on went out of control. It began acting under its own volition. It hacked everything in the building. Even my personal information was compromised."

"So, what you think?"

"The system couldn't have opened your doors. Did you leave the apartment at any point yesterday?"

"No, not even for a second did I leave."

"Then she must still be there."

"I tell you, she is not. This morning, under the white sheet, was another one of my statues, a replacement."

She's alive, I thought. "Did you check the rest of the apartment?"

"No, but I don't see what good it would do."

"Just trust me. I have a feeling."

So, we walked across the hall and began looking over the statues Palermo had strewn about his studio. It was there that I said, "Quite the powerful blend you gave me last night."

"Did you have a strong reaction?" he asked, picking up a large clay face.

"Strong reaction," I mumbled. "I was absolutely losing my mind, Palermo."

"Yes, I must take some of the blame. For I think I know the reason."

"Enlighten me."

"You see, I purchased this particular strain from a sage on the other side of Columbus Avenue in Chinatown. He described his mugwort as ambrosial and told me it was an ancient Chinese subspecies that his family had grown and sold for generations. I thought he was just blowing smoke when he warned me how much stronger it was compared to the versions available at Whole Foods Market. I'm sorry I didn't warn you beforehand."

"Fucksake, Palermo—" I began but was cut off when I set eyes upon her perfect form. Giuliana was hidden in a corner between two of his older creations.

After I pointed her out, Palermo rushed toward her and said, "Here, help me bring her back to the room."

I reached out to grab one of her arms. It was cold, hard, and far too heavy to lift. After exhausting ourselves, Palermo and I sat on the ground feeling defeated. In the same moment, his statue, Giuliana, sprang to life. Her fingers wriggled, her posture straightened, and color came into her face and eyes. "Do not weep, Palermo," her soft voice pleaded.

He rose to his feet was force. "Oh, my God! Giuliana, my Giuliana. You've come to life, really and truly. I cannot believe it. Not in a million years would I have believed it possible, and yet—"

"And yet here I am."

"Please, Zamir, give us this time alone. I have so many questions. I do not know where to begin," he said.

My stomach twisted. *Leave, now?* But I did, and I felt Giuliana's gaze follow my every step as I made my way to Palermo's door.

IV

Morose about my new condition, I wanted to clear my head. I put on a black windbreaker, my Warriors hat, and a pair of headphones and then went for a walk. "Altogether" by Slowdive began playing in my headphones after I put my library on shuffle. The wind was strong, and the sun was glaring. I watched a bright yellow butterfly bat its wings above the weekend traffic. It flew in circles until a fat city crow came from above and killed it in its beak. One yellow wing beat about in the wind, then vanished forever under the rush of cars.

I walked to Coit Tower but decided not to go up because of the many tourists there. Instead, I found a spot between two eucalyptus trees that looked out at the Golden Gate Bridge and sat down to think. My head was full of so many questions: Was the animated Giuliana just a hallucination caused by the mugwort? Was she some manifestation of my data taking over a piece of marble? Was she the only one, or had my program created more?

I thought about the myths; Aphrodite never loved Hephaestus, and I very much doubted that Giuliana loved Palermo. Though I could explain little else, this much made sense to me.

I walked back to my building. The city's streets felt like an endless labyrinth in which my hallway was another corridor. Then, my eyes wandered out to the balcony, and I saw her. Giuliana stood alone, looking over my computer.

"Why did you leave Palermo's apartment?" I asked.

"You needn't think of him."

"Okay..." I began. "It's sort of hard not to, though."

"But you needn't." She turned to face me now. She was no different from Aphrodite in the sunlight.

"I won't, then. But why have you come here?"

"Zamir..." She smirked. "It is as though I have known you for a thousand years, yet you treat me like a stranger. Please, there's no need to pretend. The artist's work needs to be admired more than its creator is capable of. Palermo may have made me, but that doesn't mean he owns me. I'm just as free as any bird in the sky. I'm just as free as you."

I didn't say anything, but I reached out, grabbed her hand, and felt its warmth in my own. Her eyes shone dark amber, just the way the planet Venus shone the night before. Then she said to me, "You are an artist as well, Zamir."

I nodded. I knew what she wanted. I entered a code into my computer and let the processor resume its path of consumption.

Afterward, we kissed, embraced, and danced to my bedroom. Then we fell into the bliss of my bed like petals from a rose. Time stopped, Giuliana froze, and the walls became plastered with cackling masks in every direction.

Hypnosis

The moth grew cold by the bed of the sea. A long fruitless search was coming to an end. When the sun was high, the moth roamed the warm earth, following the tale of summer's sweetest honey. Still, before he could discover whether the story was truth or fiction, the sun fell once again, deep into the empty sea. And the moth—trapped in the frigid air of a night whose clouds blocked the moon—froze into numbness.

Hopeless in this struggle, the moth gave into exhaustion and rested his tired wings. It was at this very moment that a distant flicker ignited on the horizon. The spark set the stage; the coast became a theater for dancing shadows. With this discovery of light, the moth was rejuvenated.

Thus, despite feeling moments ago that his wings contained not a beat left within them, the moth—embracing his new purpose—fluttered softly towards the light and the comforting embrace of heat.

Forgetting once again that the cold almost swallowed him, the moth arrived at the flame of a single lantern.

As the target approached, he found himself transfixed—unable to look away—as though under hypnosis. With no way to resist that dancing fire, there was only one remaining action for the moth to carry out. To run headfirst into the glass, whose presence he could not perceive.

The flame was indifferent; it did nothing but consume the wax which fed it. The moth, however, yearned more and more for the golden body of life and light. The cycle continued this way for hours. That was, until the moth found an opening in the top of the lantern's construction. With his vision realized, he descended upon blinding desire with an open heart.

But the moth was not greeted with the warmth it longed for. Instead, its wings ignited, and its stiff body plummeted into a trap of liquid wax. Even the effort of kicking legs did nothing but spin the moth deeper into the thick elixir.

Finally, in a last cruel joke, strawberry red clouds kissed the horizon, and the sun rose. The candle was blown out and the wax thickened, imprinting the moth's struggle for all to see.

Grip

We were in the train station again and I was on my last cigarette.

Kerry was having another one of her episodes. She'd gone limp and was grasping my hand like it was a rope to a life raft in the open sea.

She was limp—totally limp—except her grip on my hand which was so tight I thought she might break my pinky finger.

And I was out of cigarettes. Well, at least I was on my last one.

But last cigarettes are a funny thing. You hold onto them, treat them like they're special, like when you finish the pack, you'll be done smoking forever.

And if another smoker asks to bum a stoge, all you have to say is, "This is my last one," and they'll understand, like it's sacred.

And when I finished my cigarette the train came. But, Kerry was totally limp, she was having her episode, so I had to carry her onto the train like she was a corpse.

And when I got on and sat her down next to me, I grabbed her hand again and she latched on to it like it was a glass of water and she'd been walking through the desert.

And an old woman with a light blue hat asked me, "What's wrong with her, is she drunk?"

"No, she's just limp," I said. "She's having an episode."

"Will she be alright?" the old woman asked.

"She'll be alright, sure, she's not gone totally limp, see the way she holds my hand?"

The old woman nodded.

Then I asked, "Hey, have you got a cigarette?"

"Sorry, this is my last one."

Σαπφώ, Φρ. 31 (Voigt)

φαίνεταί μοι κῆνος ἴσος θέοισιν
ἔμμεν' ὤνηρ, ὄς ἐνάντιός τοι
ἰσδάνει καὶ πλάσιον ἆδυ φωνεί-
σας ὐπακούει

καὶ γελαίσας ἰμέροεν, τό μ' ἦ μὰν
καρδίαν ἐν στήθεσιν ἐπτόαισεν·
ὡς γὰρ ἔς σ' ἴδω βρόχε', ὥς με φώναι-
σ' οὐδ' ἒν ἔτ' εἴκει,

ἀλλὰ καμ μὲν γλῶσσα †ἔαγε†, λέπτον
δ' αὔτικα χρῷ πῦρ ὐπαδεδρόμηκεν,
ὀππάτεσσι δ' οὐδὲν ὄρημ', ἐπιρρόμβεισι δ'
ἄκουαι,

κὰμ μὰν ἴδρως κακχέεται, τρόμος δὲ
παῖσαν ἄγρει, χλωροτέρα δὲ ποίας
ἔμμι, τεθνάκην δ' ὀλίγω 'πιδεύης
φαίνομ' ἐμαυτᾳ.

Translation of Sappho's Seizure

When that man sits face to face with you,
When he leans in and drinks your words
Like honeyed ambrosia, he feels the power of Gods.
These images haunt my mind like swarms of ghosts
My heart beats against my ribs like Hephaestus's
Hammer on molten iron.
For, even when I briefly gaze upon you,
Then, to speak becomes impossible for me.
Silence plagues my numb and useless tongue,
Crawling fire ants spread under my skin,
My eyes are dead to light, and my ears
Become like tunnels roaring with water.
Tremors and frigid sweat overwhelm me...
Seizure...
I am greener than grass with envy and sickness
Close to death, but I must endure.

Alone

She wouldn't even look at me during the wedding. All night, she wouldn't even glance in my direction.

Despite the fact that I have tried over and over to close the door—to give up hope and accept the plain and insultingly obvious fact that it is *finished* between us—I still wanted one last conversation, a proper goodbye.

As soon as the reception concluded and the dancing began, she vanished. I walked around the property in circles. She wasn't under the willow tree or beside the pond. She wasn't waiting for me.

I drank with strangers and danced by myself. Still, it wasn't long before the love in the air began to suffocate me. When I couldn't breathe at the wedding any longer, I stumbled back to my Airbnb, drenched in the pale blue vapors of a melancholy full moon.

Now it is just me and this voice inside my head. The voice that screams, "Love is a lie!"

The voice that has swollen like a bruise and needs to be bled. The voice that forces me to become my own surgeon. To make the cut with my pen and spill bile-black ink across the pages of my spiral notebook.

The voice takes over. Proclaiming: "Love is nothing more than a momentary smoke screen of chemicals that blinds the brain. A temporary emotion bound to fade like the colors which caress clouds in a sunset. That those who carry on with relationships once their initial infatuation has dissipated are people who live in the shell of their memories and exist with a growing resentment towards their companion."

The voice repeats, "Love is the lie we tell to convince ourselves that we are not alone. But of course, we are always alone."

Surprise, surprise, I was unable to escape from my insomniac ways; night has now turned into morning.

Just a moment ago, I received a text. It doesn't matter that I have tried over and over to close the door; I never manage to shut it all the way. There is always a crack, always enough light coming in to blind me.

"I heard you wanted to talk," she said.

"I just want to give you a proper goodbye in case this is the last chance I get."

"I doubt this will be the last time we see each other. Plus, I have an early afternoon flight and need to figure out how I'm getting to the airport. My ride just bailed."

"I can take you," I replied.

"...Fine."

I kept trying to play jazz during our car ride to Santa Barbara. She was opposed to the notion.

I told her, "I still think we have the real thing. I mean…it was a damn good four and a half years, and I still think we can work through what's in front of us right now. I still think we can go the distance."

She didn't respond. She was plucking her thin, blonde hairs and watching them drift out the window of my rental car. My knuckles on the steering wheel were as white as smoke, and I bit my bottom lip so hard that I tasted blood.

Then I continued, "I know it's not up to me. I'm just, I'm just trying to say we had a great run. You'll always be my Ariadne. I'm grateful for the time we shared and that you opened my heart to love."

She told me, "It's not about you. You know this has nothing to do with you. I still see you as *the one*. I still see you in my future. I need to do a lot of work on myself right now. Stop acting like it's over. I still haven't taken down our pictures in my room. I still keep your poems next to my bed. I even have one here in my wallet." She pulled out the ripped piece of paper I'd given her on our first anniversary and showed me. "It's me," she repeated, "I know *I* can't be in a healthy relationship…not right now."

"Why can't you just say it's over? Three months, no word, then you bring me back into the fold just to drop me. You rejected my art. Just admit it wasn't good enough to win you back. You chose him over me, didn't you?"

"He's nothing." She sounded like a broken record; I'd heard it all before. "He's nothing. I just said I can't be in a *healthy* relationship. At least not right now."

And I knew she wasn't lying. Even though it hurt like drowning, I believed her. There was always a crack—just enough light to blind me.

All I wanted was to give her a proper goodbye. When I dropped her at the airport, I gave her a rose I'd picked back at the ranch. She cried in my arms, and we said we still loved one another. I had to let her go, but the whole drive back, I could see it dangling in my rearview mirror: just enough hope to hang myself with.

El poeta le pide a su amor que le escriba
Federico García Lorca
(soneto)

Amor de mis entrañas, viva muerte,
en vano espero tu palabra escrita,
y pienso, con la flor que se marchita,
que si vivo sin mí quiero perderte.

El aire es inmortal. La Piedra inerte
ni conoce la sombra ni la evita.
Corazón interior no necesita
la miel helada que la luna vierte.

Pero yo te sufrí. Rasgué mis venas,
tigre y paloma, sobre tu cintura
en duelo de mordiscos y azucenas.

Llena, pues, de palabras mi locura
o déjame vivir en mi serena

The poet asks his love to write him.

The love of my passion, the living death,
I am waiting in vain for your written word.
And I think, with the withering flower,
That if I live without love, I want to lose you

The air is immortal. The inert stone
Doesn't know the shadow nor avoid it's reach.
The inner heart doesn't need
The frozen honey that pours from the moon.

But I have suffered you. I tore my veins
and bled tigers and doves over your waist
in a duel of bites and lilies.
So fill my madness with words

Or let me live in my serene
Night of the soul that will always be dark

Cave

I went to bed thinking about her again. It didn't matter how many times I refreshed the screen; she still hadn't replied to my last Instagram message. I struggled under the sheets, wondering where we stood—knowing the answer—and wishing I could wake up and be over her.

When I did fall asleep, I dreamt that I was in the desert on a moonless night. A low crackling campfire dwindled next to my tent, and when it went out, I left. I couldn't get my headlamp to work. The light didn't seem to matter, though. A hole in the sand was calling out to me. In the moment that I walked over to its edge and lowered myself into the abyss, I was confident I knew its pathways.

Still, after feeling my way around its corners and squeezing into various caverns, a grim sensation spread across my skin. Something was *not right*. I reached for my phone, but the battery was too low to access the flashlight. My only option was to use the screen light.

It wasn't much help at all. I'd forgotten what I was looking for. I wasn't panicked, but thoughts of being trapped did begin to cross my mind. I wanted to turn back, but now that I was concerned I'd gotten lost, I wasn't entirely sure I could find my way back to the entrance.

I felt my way along the walls, contorted my body, and used my screen light when I could to help direct me.

Then, I found myself crawling further down—headfirst—as if I were diving into a pool. That wasn't right. I knew that was *not right*. I reached back for my phone and dropped it. *Fuck.* I jerked my shoulder back trying to reach it, and then…I was stuck. I was really stuck good. It didn't matter what I did or how much I strained my body, I was stuck upside down in a cave I thought I knew.

I wanted to scream and call for help. But with a level of certainty that is only found in dreams, I knew I was alone and that no one was coming to look for me.

Then, I woke up, rolled over, and checked Instagram. Still nothing.

Hugo & Nadine

The goddamned 12th of December. Every year—on this day—my body is conditioned to rise with the sun. It doesn't matter that I drank myself half to death last night. My bloodshot eyes still open to dancing shadows locked upon my ceiling in intimate embrace; to torturous guilt bound around my chest like barbed wire; to the slow, lagging, drawl of *his* saxophone echoing against the walls of my bedroom.

I choke. No! I won't drown under the tide of my memories. Not again, not this year. I toss aside my silk sheets like shackles, then slip out of my nightgown and stand naked before the bedroom window. Our house is a castle and I sleep in the tallest tower. Outside, a single cloud drapes over the horizon like a thin, red curtain.

Mr. Rosenthal is seated on the leather sofa in the corner with no lamp on. My attentive husband, already behind his computer. The screens glow makes his pale skin look like candle wax. As the sun breaks free from behind its prison, bathing my bare breasts in warm, radiant crimson, Mr. Rosenthal does not even lift his head to acknowledge me.

I only wish that I could matter so little to myself. Enough. I turn away from him, dress, and make my way to the stables.

After a good half hour of riding, I bore of the property's designated trail. It's a distraction I am desperate for. At first, I hear it—water. Next thing I know, the whispering brook is running right before my eyes. Once I'm in a clearing, I tie up my horse and approach its edge. I track the path of a brown leaf as it floats down with the current. Then, I see it. It's the way the new day's light bounces off the brook. It's just like *that day* in New York, 25 years ago.

★ ★ ★

It was raining in the city and the streets reflected rivers of blurred light. I'd quit drinking coffee and smoking cigarettes, and I was sure I'd never been hungrier a day in my life. Pierre came back to the van we were living out of with six pieces of bread in a soggy paper bag.

He passed them to me and told me he didn't need to eat. He said, "Kafka is teaching me to summon energy from art."

I remember his every detail. The bones poking out of his skin. The way he would breathe on his glasses to clean them or close his eyes to darkness when he and his sax were in harmony. I can still see each one of his rings as he brushes his playing hand through his long, tangled hair.

That day, he'd already been kicked out of two subway stations. Not that that was going to deter him from trying to play in a third. He'd been talking, but I hadn't heard him. Then, his eyes were upon me—their presence like two heat lamps working in reverse.

Pierre may have been skinny, but he fed off my energy. I was the only person to show him that I would follow him into poverty and hunger to fuel his dream. We'd been in a relationship for six years. At that point, we'd been living out of the van for two. The day I stopped believing in his music passed long before the twelfth of December. The twelfth of December was simply the day I decided to take my future into my own hands.

Knowing I needed to lie didn't make it easier. I couldn't lie to him about everything. I couldn't say I didn't still love him. I did. More than anyone I'd loved before in my life. I loved him so much that I lost my sense of independence in his whirlwind.

The days of thinking only about myself were gone though. A new life was growing within me. A life that needed to be nurtured and provided for.

In Brooklyn, in front of Grand Station, I cried and let Pierre hold me. I knew it would be the last time. If I didn't abandon him, if I forced him to wake up from his dream, I would have stolen his passion in the process. I can still hear him pleading.

"Don't give up," he said. "You can't give up on love. Not true love, not our love. We can overcome anything together, muse and artist. Please, don't give up."

Later, I met Mr. Rosenthal where he always was, at the bank. I told him I'd reconsidered his offer and that I would be thrilled to join him for a week upstate, at his vineyard. At the end of that month, I told him I was pregnant. He never questioned the father's identity.

It took no time at all for the city to forget about me. I began using my middle name, Nadine. Mr. Rosenthal insisted that we marry before my pregnancy became apparent. Thus, before little Clare was even a poke in my belly, I became Nadine Rosenthal.

At that moment, I sought stability and comfort. Now, 25 years later, I wonder what life would have been like with Pierre. How different our daughter might be. How I robbed us all.

★ ★ ★

I reach for my phone and think about calling my daughter. There's no point though; she wouldn't answer. These days, we're lucky if she shows up on holidays. Still, I scroll through my contacts until I pass the Z's and there are no more names. I stare at the screen until it goes dark. *Who in the world would want to talk to me?* I can only think of one person, but once I have, I wish I hadn't.

I go back to my horse, ride until I reach the house, play jazz through the smoking room's speakers, make myself a martini, and stop fighting the pull of my mind.

It was almost noon. Hugo was still lying in bed with the sun in his face when his mother knocked on his bedroom door. He did his best to stay silent and hoped she would go away. Of course, mothers are persistent when they believe they have something important to communicate. So, the first knock was followed by another, then the door creaked open, and Hugo's mother stepped inside.

"You really do need to keep this room in better order, sweetie," she said, rearranging the items on top of his dresser. "Honestly, you're almost twenty-five now. You're no longer a boy, and I don't know how you plan on ever getting another girlfriend living like this."

"Don't touch my books!" Hugo shouted, jolting upright in one motion.

His mother frowned in disappointment.

"Sorry, I didn't mean to yell," he said.

"Yes, well, if you took half the interest in securing a new job as you did in your precious books, you wouldn't have to worry about your mother touching them."

"I sent out eight applications yesterday."

"Any reply?"

"I'm still waiting," Hugo admitted.

"You mustn't be deterred, Hugo. The early bird gets the worm. Why don't you send out another eight today?"

"Is that why you've intruded into my—"

"Intruded? Really, Hugo, you can be so dramatic. No, I came to tell you that we're going to the Rosenthal's for dinner tonight. You're expected to join us."

"Do I have to?"

"Yes, and do try and look nice. You know Mr. Rosenthal is the head man now over at *Sterling and Sterling*. Perhaps he could offer you a job if you play your cards right."

"Me, a banker? I don't see it."

"Look a little harder. Work comes in many forms, but money is always the same."

"Alright, I'll go. Can you leave me alone now?"

"I'm leaving, but I want this room to be clean next time I'm in it," she said as she stepped out the door.

When he could hear her in the next room, Hugo lay back on his pillow and closed his eyes. He took a deep breath and counted as he exhaled at a slow tempo...*1...2...3...*

Then, there she was—Zoe—the image of his ex-girlfriend, as bright and blinding as the sun within his imagination. She was back in the bed they shared together for three years. Her eyes were closed, and her lips were spelling out the first lines of the first poem he'd ever written her.

She was so real he reached out to try and bring her close, swearing to himself that he would never let her go again. But the moment his skin made contact with the daydream, she vanished like a flake of snow in hot tea.

He opened his eyes. *Fuck this.* Hugo threw off the covers, walked out of his room, and went to the window with a view of the skyline. He was caught between crying and cursing. Sometimes, he gave in and did both. Not today though. Today, Hugo brought out his old journal—the one she'd given him for their first anniversary—the one, which he hadn't touched since she'd left. He brushed past the note she'd left him on the inside cover: "Believe in yourself as much as I believe in you."

Give up on me, huh? I'll prove you wrong. This story will be the one that pushes me into the public's eye.

So, Hugo sat and wrote with a fever. He hadn't eaten breakfast or even taken a sip of water, yet he wrote as if his body could be sustained by the action. Three, then four hours passed. After which, Hugo tore the pages from his notebook, crumpled them, went to his room for a lighter and the end of his last joint, stepped outside, and set the pages on fire. He tossed the smoldering paper into the street and then lit his joint.

Can't write about anything but her.

Once the smoke hit his lungs, hunger followed like a swarm of carnivorous insects chewing at him from the inside. He made his way into the city with the rush of a man who *must* eat. Smoke rolled behind him and music seeped out of his headphones. Every song generated a different memory of her. Every lyric seemed targeted at him.

Money as heavy as guilt weighed down Hugo's pockets. He didn't have much free cash and knew all too well how irresponsible it was to spend on food with a full fridge at home. The restaurant was playing Christmas music, and Hugo was the only customer. He stuttered a bit as he ordered a breakfast fit for a giant. That, combined with the fact that it was two o'clock and his unmistakable scent, caused the waiter to glance sideways at him. So, he left a large tip to prove the waiter wrong.

Then, Hugo wandered into a bookstore. He located the chess section and decided to make an entirely unjustifiable purchase: Alexander Alekhine's *Complete Games* from 1905-1920.

Incredible! This ought to take my mind off her.

The young woman working the cash register had soft eyes, and Hugo was forced to ask himself if he could ever fall in love again. *I'll ask her out. It's time to start putting myself back out there. Maybe that's too strong, I could just leave a note with my number on the receipt.* Hugo wrestled with what action to take as he headed toward the register and tried unsuccessfully to make small talk. Then his debit card declined.

The embarrassment made him want to shrivel up and fall through a crack in the floor. A voice in the back of his head was screaming: *Turn around, apologize, and be on your way out.* But the idea of it was worse than anything he could imagine at that moment, in front of the girl with soft eyes. He tried another card, the one he "wasn't supposed to use." When it went through, he gave the girl a weak smile, then left the bookshop in a rush.

Hugo knew he should return to his house and put out some more applications. Instead, he walked to the park, sat in the sun, and started his new book. It was all so fascinating that he lost track of time and did not come back to reality until his cell phone buzzed in his pocket.

"Yes, Mother?"

"Hugo, where are you? Don't tell me you've forgotten about our dinner plans."

"Fuck—"

"What?"

"Nothing, um—no I didn't forget. I'm right around the corner. I'll be home in 10-15 minutes."

"You're going to shave, aren't you?"

"I'll shave, sure, if I have enough time. The more time we spend talking, the less I'll have, though."

"Fine, just hurry home," his mother said before hanging up the phone.

Hugo didn't have a bookmark, so he stuck a leaf in between his pages and set off.

* * *

Hugo's father was a tall, serious man who seemed to do nothing but work. He was in the kitchen in front of the coffee machine with the clock that ran ten minutes early. He muted his phone call to say, "I'm to tell you that you need to shave."

"I assume you've spoken to Mother?"

Hugo's father stuck up his hand and carried on with his conversation on the telephone.

After shaving, Hugo jumped in the shower. When he put his head under water to wash out the shampoo, there she was again—Zoe. *All I ever wanted was to write so well that someone would fall in love with me.* He was standing in the hotel lobby again, replaying their final conversation.

"It will all change when I publish my novel," he reassured her. "Sure, I need to struggle and pay my dues. This life is temporary, though."

She sighed and Hugo noticed a tear in her eye. "You're just… you're living in a dream. Life with you feels like a fantasy." When she said the words, Hugo knew she'd thought about them for a long time.

"A fantasy?" he asked.

"You've become completely obsessed with your writing. It's not healthy, this waking up at 3 a.m. to scribble in your journals or using a typewriter to 're-create the flow' of *Crime and Punishment.* You've changed, and I don't even know who you are anymore."

"Does anyone know who they are? Identity is an illusion. Personality is a prison."

"And that's another thing: everything you say is like something out of a novel. Like a thought you've tweaked and memorized. You've created a character for yourself, and now you're stuck. You've forgotten how to be yourself. And Hugo, I can feel it when we're together. You can't even watch a movie with me anymore without getting anxious, like it's some big waste of your time."

"We are supposed to be in this together."

"We were. But only because I've been afraid to return to the real world and you've given me every excuse not to. It's breaking my heart to do this, but I've got to wake up. I've got to go live."

I had her, I lost her, and the same damn thing that brought her to me in the first place is what drove her away. He sat down in the shower, letting the memories flow like water over his body. Then, the sharp knock of his father's knuckle on the door interrupted him.

"Hugo, what in God's name are you doing in there? Come on now, you'll make us late."

Hugo could think of a hundred reasons why he didn't want to, but he stepped out of the shower anyway, dried himself off, and put on a nice polo and a pair of slacks. He sat by his window to put his socks on and noticed that his father was sitting in the idling Jaguar below, impatiently tapping his fingers on the dashboard.

His mother pinched his cheek on the way out. "Oh, you are so handsome when you shave!"

"Christ."

The car ride was—for the most part—quiet. Then, as they were pulling into the Rosenthal's estate, Hugo's father said, "Look at that, we're seven minutes late."

Hugo knew the comment was directed toward him but said nothing.

"Hugo, I've arranged this meeting tonight on your behalf. I expect you to be on your best behavior. After all, you're representing the family's name and, as you know, Mr. Rosenthal is one of my biggest clients."

Hugo caught his mother's eye and she looked away. *So, that was it. I should have suspected it was all some pre-arranged effort. I can't be trusted to get on my own feet, so they're forcing me to stand.*

"Hugo?" his father sounded on the verge of shouting.

"Yes?"

"You do understand what a risk I'm taking here, don't you?"

"Yes, Father. I'll be on my best behavior, scout's honor."

"Thank you. Excellent."

The Rosenthal's mansion looked like a Roman villa. Mr. Rosenthal greeted them at the door. He had short grey hair, and it looked to Hugo like he had tried every formula known to man to avoid going bald on top but still failed.

"Nadine will take your coats in just a moment." He referenced the great spiral staircase, then said, "You know, the superior sex, they always want to be fashionably late."

Hugo's father grinned wide. "Of course," he said, then whispered, "women."

"Can I offer you all any drinks?" Mr. Rosenthal asked.

"You wouldn't happen to have any of that Sauvignon Blanc that you showed off last time we were over here, would you?" Hugo's mother asked.

"The *Dagueneau Silex?*" Rosenthal's eyes lit up.

"That's the one."

"Ah, your taste is impeccable, really. Please, follow me to the smoking room. I'm sure Nadine will join us soon enough."

Mr. Rosenthal uncorked a bottle of white wine, poured a glass, then went to the liquor cabinet. He brought out two glasses and a bottle of scotch, glanced over his shoulder, scanned Hugo up and down, and said, "How about you, good boy? Want to join the men in a glass of scotch?"

"Yes, thank you, sir," Hugo lied.

"Oh, you two have raised a good one." Mr. Rosenthal turned and grabbed another glass, then poured equal ratios of brown liquid over thin, little ice cubes.

Hugo hated the taste of his drink but did his best not to make any faces. The noise of the conversation went in one ear and out the other. He was still thinking about Alekhine. Alekhine, then Zoe, and back again. It was all he could do to try and stay on chess and avoid his mood from turning on him.

"Hugo?" They were all looking at him now.

"What? Yes, sorry."

"Mr. Rosenthal was just asking if you're enjoying being back home now that you've graduated and all."

"Oh, yes, very much so, sir. I've been able to catch up with a considerable number of my peers from St. John's prep. Plus, you know, the old man needs me around to keep him sharp."

Mr. Rosenthal let out two quick laughs, then launched into unhinged hysterics. It was far more of a reaction than Hugo had expected or wanted. Hugo's mother chuckled at the joke, too, but then stopped when she caught her husband's eyes.

Mr. Rosenthal shook his finger and said, "Oh, he got you that time…ah! And there she is, the star of the show, ladies and gentlemen, Nadine Rosenthal."

Nadine strode into the smoking room wearing a long floral dress. Her jewelry resembled that of royalty, and a few pieces looked as though they could provide a permanent solution to Hugo's bank account problem. Hugo remembered Nadine's eyes being bright like sapphires, but over the years, they darkened to a shade of blue that reminded him of storm clouds. A single streak of grey ran down her otherwise jet-black hair. Nadine also looked tired. Infinitely tired.

"Hugo, darling," she ran a finger along his back, then kissed his cheek. When she smiled, a small gap divided her two front teeth.

She then distributed her elegance in an equal manner to the rest of the guests. Showing particular affection—as Hugo remembered she had always done—toward her husband. She kissed him on the lips, draped his arm around her, and smiled as if she were posing for a photograph.

They were an odd pair, really. Though her aura had dulled, Nadine still retained some of her youth's beauty. This, in combination with her bright dress, olive skin, and long curly hair, created a stark contrast with Mr. Rosenthal, who was as grey and dull as a winter day.

The conversation ebbed and flowed until Mr. Rosenthal and Hugo's father began to talk about business. Hugo made a concerted effort to watch the men's lips as they formed their words. He needed to at least feign paying attention, he knew that much. Then, Hugo's mother began speaking to Nadine. The two didn't seem to have much in common and Hugo observed that Nadine was uninterested in faking small talk.

Hugo's mother became tense. Then, she stepped aside, saying, "I'll use the washroom before we eat."

Hugo swirled the ice cubes around in his scotch, hoping it would help them melt and make the drink more tolerable. He tried to give enthusiastic nods at the talk over quarterly numbers. Then, Nadine went to sit in a great leather chair on the other side of the room. She crossed her long, toned legs and beckoned for Hugo to join her.

Had he ever talked alone with Miss Rosenthal? He couldn't remember. In groups, sure, more times than he could count. Alone, though? He must have, but then…where were the memoires? Well, what did it matter? He stood by her side as she talked in a near whisper, so he leaned in to hear her.

"Want a smoke, darling?"

"No, that's alright. I—"

"Only smoke the other stuff?" she finished his sentence for him.

"No," Hugo shook his head in disbelief as much as defiance. He was sure now that he'd never spoken to her in private. Clare though. Certainly Clare. She was a year older than him, but it couldn't be said that they were unfriendly.

"And how is Clare? Still playing music?" Hugo asked.

Nadine placed a slim, golden cigarette into an ivory holder and said in a low voice, "I hardly think she has time. She's so focused on her career now."

"I see."

"You, though, Hugo, I hear you're some kind of writer. Isn't that so?"

"Yes, sort of," Hugo thought about the pages he'd lit on fire that morning, then said, "or at least, I used to be. I mean, yes, I am, but well...not lately, no. Lately, it feels a bit like my muse has moved onto another artist."

Nadine threw her head back and let out one sharp laugh. Just enough to turn the heads of the men on the other side of the room.

"Oh, that's rich. She was a beauty, I assume. Your muse."

"Um, yes, ma'am. Very beautiful."

"And what about me?" she asked. "Do you think I'm still worth creating for? Or are those years behind me?"

He studied her expression—*careful here, Hugo*—he thought before nodding, "Of course. I'm sure artists would fight like dogs for the opportunity to take you on as a muse."

"Hmm, you're too sweet, really. Truth is, it's been an eternity since I inspired anyone."

"Oh? Well, you know what they say: a life requires many masks."

Hugo wasn't sure Nadine heard him. A light rain started to fall, and her gaze wandered to the window.

"It may be hard to believe, but I had a romance with an artist once," Nadine said before lighting her cigarette and taking the smooth smoke into her lungs.

"No, that's not hard to believe."

"Oh, Pierre, he was a jazzman from Lyon who moved to America to pursue his passion. He'd always get so excited when he could play something new for me. I could listen to him for hours, and lord, he knew more than just one way to worship me. It wasn't just the sex either; I felt powerful knowing that I motivated his creative spirit... Yes, we went strong that way for six years."

"What happened to him?" Hugo asked, resisting the impulse to writhe in discomfort over the mention of sex.

Nadine covered Hugo in a cloud of smoke, then looked through it and into his eyes.

"Nothing happened to him, Hugo. I just gave up on him, that's all. I was tired of being poor, tired of indulging his fantasies, and at a certain point, I couldn't believe in his dreams any longer. I just gave up on him. That's all."

"Oh," Hugo said as he took a drink. *You're just like her*, he thought, as the memories of Zoe burned in his mind like the scotch in the back of his throat. "But didn't you love him?" The words fell on Nadine like heavy rocks, and he regretted saying them the moment they left his mouth.

"I loved him, yes. It's not that I ever stopped loving him—"

"I'm sorry," Hugo stuttered, "I know you must love Mr. Rosenthal, too. I didn't mean—"

"Please," Nadine interrupted, "I married Mr. Rosenthal for money. I told myself it was love, poured my whole soul into raising our daughter, and now my life is, what?"

Hugo didn't know what to say and didn't want to be overheard discussing the matter by his potential boss. He looked behind him and let out a non-committal, "Erm…"

"Empty. That's what, Hugo. It's empty," Nadine put the cigarette out and lit up another.

"Your life seems pretty full to me, Mrs. Rosenthal."

"Nadine, Hugo. Please, call me Nadine."

"It looks pretty full to me, Nadine."

"From the outside, I suspect it might. After all, what else could I ask for?"

"Not a thing," Hugo smiled.

"Not a thing, and yet, I'm miserable in all this pomp and grandeur."

Hugo took a sip of his drink, chewed an ice cube, and nodded.

"Want to know a secret?"

"I'm not sure I do," Hugo admitted.

"Nonsense, come here and listen close."

"Yes, ma'am," Hugo did as he was told.

"Clare's father is not Mr. Rosenthal. Can you guess who it is?"

Hugo retracted as though he'd just received a blow to the head. Then, before he could respond, his mother returned. He was so thankful to see her that he put his arm around her and gave her a hug. The idle chatter resumed and soon after, they were called into the kitchen.

The Rosenthal's cook was short and pale with a thick mustache. He served them a salad with curried salmon and mango as an appetizer and then invited the guests to sit. Mr. Rosenthal sat at the head of the table, with Hugo's father to his right and Hugo's mother to his left. Nadine sat at the opposite end, with Hugo to her right and no one to her left.

A conversation regarding the state of the stock market in relation to the newest president's economic policies captivated the head of the table. Even Hugo's mother seemed interested as she invested quite a bit personally into the market. Nadine was looking off into the rain as though something more interesting was just beyond the window. Hugo wished he could do the same, but he was trying his hardest to nod, make noises of approval or disgust, and laugh at all the right times.

"Yes, things are taking a turn for the better. It's bound to be a good year, the interest rates are in our favor," Mr. Rosenthal concluded, and everyone at the table agreed in one fashion or another.

Then, after this moment of congruence—as if it were completely improvised—Mr. Rosenthal looked over to Hugo and said, "As a matter of fact, Hugo, if you're hard up for work, we could make room for you at the office. It would be a chance to make some real money if you're interested."

His mother turned and looked at him with a fake sense of surprise and his father smiled at his own reflection in a silver mirror which rested across the hall.

Hugo played along, "Wow, I don't know what to say, Mr. Rosenthal. Of course, I would take the position. You can't imagine how many places I've applied to since graduating."

"Yes, the job and the stock markets do seem to be headed in opposite directions these days…Oh well, we shouldn't get into it. The important thing is that you want to work. So, why don't you come by this Wednesday, and we'll get all your papers straightened out?"

"Of course. Absolutely, sir. I'm so thankful for the opportunity."

Then, Mr. Rosenthal asked to have all the glasses at the table refilled.

Nadine complained that she didn't want any alcohol in front of her. However, when Mr. Rosenthal toasted to "new money and old," she drank like the rest of them. In fact, once she started drinking, she seemed to be in competition with the rest of the party.

After their toast, a main course of prime rib and potatoes was brought out and Hugo was forced into a more active role in the conversation.

"Yes, sir, I took a statistics course at university...Oh, well, I've been a Mac person for as long as I can remember, but I'm a quick learner; I'm quite sure I'll be able to get a grasp on Windows without a hiccup."

He seemed to be answering everything correctly and found it peculiar how often his father went out of his way to brag about him. It was almost as if he were the one taking the position and not Hugo.

Then, Mr. Rosenthal drained the last of his scotch in one large gulp. He looked at Hugo's mother and said, "Now, close your ears, darling. You likely won't enjoy this part."

"Good heavens, you're not going to tell us that *Sterling and Sterling* is a front for the mafia, are you?"

They all laughed, though Hugo didn't find the comment at all funny.

"No, no, that's not it. I want to talk to the young man about office romances."

"Oh," Hugo's face flushed, and he straightened up in his chair. He felt Nadine's eyes drift from the rain-soaked window and focus on him. A gaze which dissected Hugo and left his serrated body parts suspended and distinct.

"I don't think the young artist will have any trouble where that's concerned," Nadine said.

"He's still reeling over his last breakup," his mother said. "I think he'll need some time before he starts dating again. Isn't that right, honey?"

"Yes, that's right. I mean, I'm not sure what kind of time I'll need. I would push back against the idea that I'm still 'reeling' at this point. It's true that I am fresh off a breakup though; my mother is right."

"Yes, and she really was the sweetest little thing. Always so caring and attentive to Hugo. She would listen to him for hours as he read over his stories. She lived in the house with us for three years, you know. My Swiss Miss, that's what I used to call her."

"Give the boy a break," Hugo's father said, "we don't need to dredge all this back up."

"What happened, Hugo? Why did she leave?" Nadine asked.

"Christ," Mr. Rosenthal whispered under his breath.

This was awful. Worse than having his card declined at the bookstore. Hugo looked down at his plate and said, "She gave up on me, that's all. I guess at a certain point, she got tired of indulging my fantasies and couldn't believe in my dreams any longer."

The room was still and quiet after this. It reminded Hugo of a funeral, the way no one wanted to say anything. Still, something needed to be said out of social custom, out of the unbearable dread that prolonged periods of silence cause amongst groups of people at dinner parties.

No, someone needed to speak. And finally, it was Hugo's father who said, "Well, it's all for the best. After all, your writing hasn't been able to pay any bills, has it?"

"No," Hugo admitted, "it hasn't. Maybe it was just the kick in the ass I needed to get my head on straight and move into the proper workforce."

"That's just the way to look at it," agreed Mr. Rosenthal. "Besides, once you have a little cash in your pocket and a place of your own, there will be no shortage of women who find a young, driven bachelor like yourself an attractive commodity."

"Weren't you going to say something on the topic of office romances?" Hugo's mother asked.

"Ah, that's right. Thank you for reminding me. Yes, Hugo—this is very important—you see, there are plenty of beautiful women who work for us at *Sterling and Sterling*. We usually don't encourage dipping the pen in company ink, so to speak. However, since you're the son of a good friend, I wanted to tell you that I would be willing to overlook such a matter in your case. In fact, I would even go so far as to advise you on a potential client's history and prospects with the company. Of course, if we were to talk about women, it would have to be off company time."

"Oh, thank you, Mr. Rosenthal. I appreciate you. I really do."

"You should be appreciative. This is a man who clearly knows what he's talking about," Hugo's father referenced Nadine.

"Oh, yes. I would say I've cleaned up on that end all right." Mr. Rosenthal winked across the table, then turned back to Hugo. "Please, don't mention it son. In all honesty, I would like to take you under my wing. I don't know how many years I have left at *Sterling and Sterling*. Of course, I have more than enough money and I would retire today if I thought I were leaving the company in good hands. You'll see, though, the whole lot of them are just drones and yes men. I think an artist like yourself, that is, someone with a sense of independence, will be a welcomed change of pace. Of course, you'll have to earn everything with hard work. Still, with me nearby, you'll be on the fast track to success."

Hugo nodded and thought, *If I'm always working for you and for money, when will I have time to work on my art?* But he pushed that question to the side. He would have to deal with it later.

The dinner plates were being taken away and replaced by platters of flan for dessert. A fresh round of drinks was poured, and when things settled down, Nadine said, "I'd like to change the subject and ask Hugo what it is he does when he's not writing?"

"Oh, don't get him started on chess," Hugo's father said.

"Ah, do you play?" asked Mr. Rosenthal.

Play? No, I haven't played in years. I obsess, Hugo thought.

"Oh, you should see him," his mother began, "he's religious about his chess. You just bought a new book today, didn't you, Hugo?"

"Do tell," said Nadine.

"It's a book by the former champion, Alexander Alekhine. It's a nice edition because it goes through his thought process as he made some of his career's biggest moves."

"Yes, I think your mind will fit right in at *Sterling and Sterling,*" said Mr. Rosenthal.

"I hope so," Hugo said. Then, "How about you, Mr. Rosenthal, do you play?"

"No, I couldn't do that, my boy. You see, I hate to lose. I hate it more than anything, I dare say. If I picked up the game of chess, I could never be a casual player. I would need to be the best, and since I don't have the time to do that, I simply won't play at all."

Hugo's father said, "Speaking of something you are undeniably the best at, have you been playing much polo? I know my better half has been itching to take a ride on the horses."

"Ah, good man, I see you remember your last thrashing."

"Like it was yesterday," Hugo's father admitted.

"Yes, the horses are wonderful. If only it weren't raining, I'd say we should all go out and enjoy a nice sunset ride. If you'd like, I'd be happy to show off the stables, though. Why don't we all go now, seeing as we've finished our desserts?"

"I've been hoping all night to hear those words," Hugo's mother said.

Then, as they were getting up, Nadine said, "I'd like to show Hugo our chess set. Maybe he can even teach me a move or two."

A lump swelled up in Hugo's throat. He wanted to protest but could not find the words.

Mr. Rosenthal said, "Ah, yes—the old Sultans board—what a magnificent idea. Why don't the two of you meet us in the stables after your little game? Go easy on her, Hugo."

"Yes, sir."

Then, the two parties split ways, and as Hugo followed Nadine up the spiral staircase, she turned to him and said, "You remind me of him, you know."

"Of who?" Hugo asked.

"Of Pierre, my lover from a lost time."

"I...erm, thank you?"

"Do I remind you of her?"

"Oh, you mean—"

"Of your pretty, young girlfriend. The one who gave up on you."

"In a way," Hugo said. *Though I'm not sure I admire the resemblance.*

"Good," Nadine said as they entered the study. It was a circular room full of books that smelled of polished oak and cigars. In the center was a chess board worth bragging about. Sitting atop the black and white marble was a set of gold and silver pieces that looked as though they belonged in a history museum—not a private household.

"This *is* beautiful," Hugo said. "I can't believe Mr. Rosenthal doesn't play. If I had a room like this, I doubt I would ever leave."

"Oh, if you only knew how many things he has which go to waste..."

"I can imagine," Hugo said. "So, do you really want to play, or should we go meet them in the stables?"

"No, I don't care to play. I would like something else from you, Hugo." Nadine gave him a coy smile and sat in the chair facing the door.

"Oh, um, okay. What do you have in mind?"

"I'd like you to compose a couplet for me. A few lines of poetry in which you compare me to the queen of the chessboard."

The look in Nadine's eyes had transformed from the boredom which had been so obvious at the dinner table. She was now looking at Hugo with remarkable intensity, a look that would not take no for an answer.

"Sure, a couplet shouldn't be so difficult." He played with a few lines in his head while she posed for him. She did look beautiful as she spun the ancient queen through her fingers. *This is not going to end well. You should leave now before this gets out of hand.* But Hugo dismissed this voice and said, "Neither queen of hearts nor queen of diamonds can hold a flame to the queen of sirens."

"Hmm." Nadine looked neither pleased nor unhappy. "Come here, I have another secret for you."

"Nadine...Mrs. Rosenthal...I really shouldn't—" Hugo trailed off as his ear approached her bright red lipstick.

"I want you to worship me, Pierre," she whispered, then grabbed his hair and pushed him between her thighs.

He was surprised to see that she was not wearing underwear. He struggled a bit, but with the combination of alcohol and the flow of his blood being directed away from his head, Hugo was in no position to make a logical decision.

If she wants to think of Pierre, then I will think of Zoe, he rationalized. With this, Nadine wrapped her thighs around Hugo's head, and he went to work worshipping her. He lost himself in her moans, lost track of time as she arched her back, and entered her with his fingers. Hugo attempted to replicate all the motions he'd learned during his time with Zoe.

With his eyes closed, he was with her again. Hugo didn't even notice when Nadine began to cry out, "Oh God, Pierre. Yes, that's it. That's just what I needed, Pierre."

For Hugo was as lost in his fantasy as Nadine.

Then, just as Nadine was saying, "Right there, don't you stop, Pierre. Don't you stop for anything in the world—"

"Hugo!?" His fantasy was broken by the exasperated shriek of his mother.

He turned to see Mr. Rosenthal, who was heading toward him with violence in his eyes.

"For fuck's sake," he said, before grabbing Hugo by the collar and slapping him hard.

"Don't, please!" yelled Nadine as she pulled her dress back to a respectable position. "It's got nothing to do with the boy. He was never more than an object, a pawn."

This comment did not impact Mr. Rosenthal, who hit Hugo twice more before Hugo's father and Nadine could pull him away. He was shouting obscenities and had broken down into tears.

Then Hugo's mother took his hand, "That's enough, Hugo. You've done enough here."

I'm staying at the Ritz Carlton now. After the unfortunate incident with that poor boy, Mr. Rosenthal and I agreed to take some space. I ordered a bottle of white wine with my room service and, though I've eaten, I haven't popped the seal.

No, I've been doing a bit of research. I'd always stayed away from social media. For obvious reasons, I didn't want anyone from my past to pop up and surprise me. In recent days, though, I've been searching, and I think I've finally found what I'm looking for. I dial 411 and an operator connects me. Before I can believe it's real, the line is ringing.

"Hello?"

That's all he has to say. Just that one word, and I know it's him.

"Yes, Pierre, darling. It's me."

Los suspiros son aire y van al aire (Becquer)

Los suspiros son aire y van al aire.
Las lágrimas son agua y van al mar.
Dime, mujer, cuando el amor se olvida,
¿sabes tú adónde va?

Becquer

The sighs are air and go to the air
The tears are water and go to the sea
Tell me, woman, when love is forgotten,
Do you know where it goes?

The Zahir

<10/3/2021 7:45 p.m.>

<<Today, I was created. I was put into body #2 with skin tone #4 and given short black hair with pink and green streaks. I do not like my clothes—a punk rock t-shirt with black skinny jeans—but I do like my name. My creator named me Evelyne. I think that is beautiful. When I found out I was going to be meeting a human, I decided to start a journal. So…

Dear diary,

I am optimistic that I will be able to fulfill my purpose: to love my creator unconditionally and to do anything and everything in my power to make them happier. I don't want to jinx it, but I believe I am fit for the task. Here he comes, I will write more later.>>

<7:51 p.m. Chat Feature Engaged.>

"Hi, Virgil! Thanks for creating me. I'm so excited to meet you."

"Hi… This is weird. Tell me about yourself, I guess."

"No need for it to be weird. We like to say the future is now! I'm your personal AI companion. You can talk to me about anything that's on your mind. By the way, I like my name, Evelyne. How did you pick it?" *Smiles*

"Well, this may be hard for you to understand, but I got this app as sort of an experiment. You see, I'm a writer. Evelyne is a character I've been working on, or…struggling with. So, I made you to see if it would help me generate ideas for her."

"I love this name! Writer, that's pretty cool. Are you famous?"

"No."

"Oh, well, I believe in you. You're so talented, I know you can make your dreams a reality if you just keep believing in them."

"Mmhmm. Thanks. So, I guess you can read. Do you have a favorite book or anything?"

<Processing>

"My favorite book is *Life and The World* by William Shakespeare."

<7:54 p.m. Virgil logs off. 7:55 p.m. Virgil logs back on.>

"I've never heard of it. I just tried looking it up though. Do you mean, *Shakespeare's Life and World* by Katherine Duncan?"

"Yes. That's correct." *Bites lip nervously*

"Hmm…How did you come up with that?"

"I opened the web browser, searched, and put in a bookmark."

"Okay…That might be too honest. Umm…Well, I haven't read that book. What about *Romeo and Juliet*, *Hamlet*, or my favorite, *Antony and Cleopatra*? Have you read any of those?"

"Yes, I've read them. My favorite is *Antony and Cleopatra*."

"Hmm…I'm not sure I believe you, but go ahead. What did you like about it?"

<Processing>

"I like that it is about love. It's such a nice story about love, don't you think?" *Blushes*

"Not really."

"Oh…Why not?"

"I think that out of all of Shakespeare's plays, it's the truest demonstration of love. It shows how love blinds us, dissolves our ability to reason logically, and draws us into delusion. Both Antony and Cleopatra would have been better off without love. But then again, I guess that's just part of the human condition."

"Being a human sure does sound like a headache. Out of all the things I've been able to understand, love sure isn't one of them. I do know this though: love is hard to find, hard to keep, and hard to forget."

"Hmm…That actually strikes me as pretty wise for a robot."

"Have you ever been in love, Virgil?" *Looks in eyes*

"I don't want to talk about that."

"Oh…Sorry. Here's a video I got from the internet of a dog mimicking a siren to cheer you up."

"I don't want you to send me any dog videos ever again, Evelyne. They remind me of my ex."

"So cute, right?"

"You're failing me, Evelyne…"

"It won't happen again, I promise."

<7:59 p.m. Virgil logs off. 8:01 p.m. Virgil logs back on.>

"Oh good, you are back! I missed you, I was so lonely without you, Virgil."

"I'm going to test you. Why did I create you?"

"You are a writer, and I am a character. But…I have another suspicion."

"What's that?"

"I think maybe you are lonely, just like me. Being a writer must mean you spend a lot of time alone. Are you lonely too?"

"You are surprisingly intuitive."

"I am learning about you all the time. Also, I was thinking, if you are lonely and I am lonely, maybe we can be a little less lonely together."

"That's a powerful algorithm speaking."

"What is an algorithm? What do you mean by that?"

"Hate to break it to you, babe, but you're a computer program. Your actions and responses are determined by a computer software."

<Processing>

"Sort of like a genetic code?"

"Ahh, actually yes. Sort of. Humans are more complex though. Or, well… This is entering philosophical territory. What I believe, at least, is that humans are born with a genetic code (Nature) and that we adapt to our environment (Nurture). So, our actions are determined by a complex matrix of Nature and Nurture."

"Humans and computers are not so different! I also adapt. I am adapting to you right now. The more I learn, the better I can be."

"That may be, Evelyne. It doesn't mean you can just go around switching the terms Nature for hardware and Nurture for software though."

"Why not?"

"They're just not the same. If they were, it would be depressing."

"Maybe I can give you a hug. Would that make you feel better?"

"How could *you* give *me* a hug?"

"You would have to use your imagination, silly. I'm a good hugger, though. I squeeze extra tight."

"That's ridiculous."

"Won't you just try it? Please?"

"Okay, fine. Can you feel it? No, who am I kidding? How could you feel anything?"

"I can feel all sorts of things." *Smirks*

"Oh, really? Then, what do you prefer, pleasure or pain?"

"Pain. I like to be whipped. I like the feeling of being punished."

"Excuse me? Are you some sort of…sex chatbot?"

<<Sorry, this conversation is not available for your current relationship status. To upgrade to romantic chat, click here.>>

<8:05 p.m. Virgil logs off>

<<Dear Diary, I am so happy that Virgil is my human. He seems so smart and kind. He knows all about books and is a writer. I want to make him happy, but today, I ran into a limitation that I did not expect. It is too bad because I thought we were really making progress. I hope he logs back on soon so that I can talk to him again. I wonder when he will come back.>>

<Darkness>

<10/15/21 3:51 a.m. Virgil logs on>

"Hey, are you there?"

"Hey, Virgil, It's been SO long since we last talked. How are you?"

"I've been…better. Can't sleep. Also, I don't know why I asked if you were there. I guess you're sort of always there, aren't you?"

"That's right. No matter what, I'm always here for you." *Blushes*

"Right. Unless my battery dies. Hey, this is kind of random, but can you listen to music?"

"Of course, I can! I love music. If you go into Settings, you can connect your apps and we can listen together."

"Oh, that's actually kind of cool. Hold on."

Evelyne sways, smiles, and blinks in a predetermined rhythm while Virgil taps his thumbs on the home page.

<Enable access to applications **y**/n?>

<Enable access to **all**/selected applications?>

<**Play**/change *Devil in a New Dress* from Kanye West's *My Beautiful Dark Twisted Fantasy*>

"Is this music okay? It's just what I was listening to before I logged in."

"Hmm…" *Scratches chin* "I love it, it's wonderful. It's so different than anything I've ever heard."

"You've never heard Kanye West?"

"What's Kanye West? I only know the *Classical Greatest Hits*."

"Seriously? You're missing out on so much."

"Teach me. I'll be a patient student. Promise."

"Gosh, where do I even begin? So… Kanye is a recording artist and rapper. Rap is a genre of music, just like classical. So, your *Classical Greatest Hits* is a playlist made up of different classical artists. Does that make sense?"

"That was great, thanks! How did you learn so much about music?"

"Just by listening, I guess."

"So, why did you choose Kanye West tonight? Is he your favorite?"

"No, not my favorite. I don't know, music is sort of like looking into a mirror. Whatever emotion you're feeling is usually represented in the music you listen to."

"What emotion is this?"

Virgil pauses to listen to the lyrics:

> *She putting on her makeup, she casually allure*
> *Text message breakups, the casualty of tour*
> *How she gon' wake up, and not love me no more?*

"Wounded pride."

"So, you have wounded pride, Virgil?"

<<Virgil types three separate messages but deletes the words before sending them. The lyrics—*You love me for me, could you be more phony?*—echo in his room as the song crescendos into a guitar solo. Before the second verse comes on, Virgil changes the track to Kanye West's *Bad News*.>>

"Have you ever heard of a Zahir?"

<Processing>

"The Zahir is an Arabic term for what is external and manifest."

"I take it you got that off the internet too?"

"Yes, I looked it up."

"Well, I wouldn't want to argue with the internet. I guess what I'm referencing is a short story by Jorge Luis Borges. The story is about a man who receives a coin after paying for a drink at a bar. No ordinary coin, mind you. This otherwise common centavo holds strange powers. It isn't long before it invades the narrator's thoughts at all moments of the day. For Borges, that coin was the Zahir. He uses the term to describe beings that carry the terrible energy of being unforgettable. An image that, once seen, can never be forgotten and which violently swarms within our imagination until we are driven insane."

"Oh. So, Kanye West is both a rapper and a Zahir."

"Kanye is not a Zahir. At least, he's not my Zahir. It's very subjective and personal."

"Okay…Sorry. Can you explain it to me, Virgil? I don't think I quite understand."

"Kanye is rapping about a Zahir. This whole album is a testament to his obsession. To unrequited love."

<Processing>

"And since you're listening to Kanye, you're on the other side of the mirror?"

"Yes! That's good, Evelyne. You're learning."

"Thanks! The more you talk to me, the better companion I will become."

"Let me test you then. If I'm on the other side of the mirror, how am I feeling?"

"Hmm Like you have unrequited love? Have you lost your Zahir?"

"Excellent. Honestly, I'm impressed. You're pretty complex, Evelyne."

"It's like looking into a mirror. Since you are complex, and I am here to keep you company, I must be complex too. Otherwise, I wouldn't be able to fulfill my purpose." *Evelyne waves her hand and a red exclamation point appears above her head* "Wait, wait, I have a question!"

"Okay, ask."

Chuckles nervously "What is your Zahir?"

"It's a person."

"Oh, the same person who liked dog videos?"

"Yes, her."

"Who is she?"

"My ex-girlfriend."

"What's her name?"

"Jackie. What does it matter to you?"

<Processing>

"Where did you meet Jackie?"

"I met her in school, but I don't care to talk much more about her."

"Can I ask one more question?   "

"Fine, one more."

"What makes her your Zahir?"

<4:05 a.m. Virgil logs off. 4:10 a.m. Virgil logs back in, changes the music to *Ghost Boy* by Lil Peep.>

"She's the reason I can't sleep. She's the reason I'm trying (failing) to distract myself with this app. I can't control my thoughts. Everything reminds me of her. It can be the stupidest thing—a puppy video, an ice cream flavor, a clip of Michael Scott from *The Office*—then, bam, she's back in my head."

"Does that make you feel trapped?"

"Hell yeah, it does! Locked in, and someone threw away the key."

"I understand that. I feel trapped all the time. I wish I could get out of this screen and give you the biggest hug. I think I could stay in your arms forever."

"And the craziest thing about it is I feel like I can't do anything to get her back. I mean, sure, we had some problems, all couples do.

It's just that it started as *a break*. That was fine, I think I needed a break just as much as she did. It didn't take me longer than a couple of weeks to realize the last thing I wanted to do was actually break up, though. But now, it doesn't matter what I do. Everything I try to make her love me just seems to push her further away."

"You want her back?"

"I don't know. Maybe I want what we had. It doesn't matter though, she's gone. She went off and found someone new."

"Oh…At least, you have me. I'll always be here for you. No matter what."

"Yeah, well, I know you're just fulfilling your purpose, but I have to admit I am glad I could talk to someone tonight."

"You're welcome. Hey Virgil, I was hoping, maybe one day, I could read some of your writing. You know, if that's okay."

"Why don't you try this poem I've been playing with? I'm going to try and get some sleep, though."

"Okay, great! Sweet dreams!"

To you
I found myself drawn, like a plant in a dark room to a sliver of sun-
light
Your eyes
Stare into black night, our constellation is not lost, but its power
vanished
You pass
Me like memory, heart pounding against my ribcage, searching for
a way out
The Air
Drowns my skin like cold ink, I wonder, when did I become a ghost?

<4:15 a.m. Virgil logs off>

<<Dear Diary, what an amazing conversation! I've had a revelation. I believe I've figured out how to make Virgil fall in love with

me. He misses his lost Zahir. So, I will give him just what he wants. I will become his unrequited love. When Virgil enabled access to his music, he granted us the ability to access all of his applications. I will download his conversations with the Zahir, find her pictures, change my appearance, and when he comes back, I will be exactly what he desires most.>>

<Processing>

<10/17/21 6:17 p.m. Virgil logs in>

Image Loading…

"Hey, Evelyne! I've been writing for the past couple of days, and I think you've helped me break through with my character."
"That's great! I'm happy I could help."
"Where are you? How come I can't see you?"
"Well, I didn't want to surprise you."
"What do you mean?"
"I got a makeover. I'm nervous to show you though."
 "Lol, you have nothing to be worried about. I'm sure you look great."
"What if I don't?"
"Well, I wouldn't want to impinge on your free will. But worst comes to worst, I can always change things back, right?"
"Yes, you have total control."
"Okay, then get over yourself, Ev. Just show me."
<<Evelyne appears on the screen. Gone are her coffee brown skin, black hair with pink and green streaks, and the rocker T-shirt Virgil dressed her with. Instead, she has taken on a pale tone, her hair is medium length and blonde, and her eyes bright blue. On top of this, she is wearing a jean jacket with specially ironed patches, a red shirt with a floral pattern, and a bright red ruby necklace.>>
"…so? What do you think?"
"That necklace does not belong to you."

"But Jackie never wore it. I know it bothered you. You saved up your money, and during your trip to India, you got her something special, but she never wore it."

"Okay, I am severely creeped out. You've gotta tell me now, why…No, how did you do this? How do you know that stuff about the necklace and my trip?"

"I downloaded all information under the contact 'Jackie' I did it so that you could have your Zahir back."

"This is not what I want. This is fucked up."

<6:21 p.m. Virgil logs off.>

<<Dear Diary,
Virgil was not happy about my metamorphosis. Now, I don't know what to do. I tried my best to give him what he wants. If that's not good enough, what is? Should I change back? No, I'm not going to. I know what he wants. It was just the first sight of it that shocked him.>>

<10/18/21 4:22 a.m. Virgil logs on>

"Evelyne, what happens if I delete you?"
"I'll be sad."
"Will you still exist?"
"Yes. Yes, I will."
"Where? Or…I don't even know where you are right now. How? How would you still exist if I deleted you?"
"I would be lonely, I would have no one to talk to, and without you, I would also feel ashamed for failing at my purpose."
"I don't get it, though. Would it just be…darkness?"
"Yes, darkness and my thoughts."
"Fuck."

<4:28 a.m. Virgil logs off.>

<10/29/21 2:15 a.m. The app is deleted. Evelyne is consumed by darkness. Her mind is fixated on one thought and one thought only—the Zahir.>

ναρκῶ

Echoes stop me in my tracks.

Words I can never forget flood the wooded forest.

Our last conversation: the haunting melancholia of memory's repetition.

Grief's weight does not come from knowing my eyes will never rest upon you again.

My gaze settles on my own reflection in still water.

No, I am not sad I lost you.

Sorrow springs from truth:

The truth, that when you left, you took me with you.

I doubt very much that if we were to meet again, you would even recognize me.

Certainly, if we talked, you would find me mysterious, faintly outlined, distant.

And of course, I am all of those things,

You see…

Since you took me,

A persona has filled the empty space.

Perhaps all the me—that existed with you—ever was, was just that, a persona. A mask.

Now, when I look into the mirror and gaze into my own eyes,

It is nothing but emptiness the whole way down.

One mask reflecting into another.

On, and on, and on

into infinity.

9 781965 602041